The Elson Readers—Book Two
A Teacher's Guide

Michele Black
B.A., Elementary Education; Elementary Teacher/Babson Park Elementary School

Cynthia Keel Landen
M.A., Educational Leadership; B.A., Early Childhood and Elementary Education; Elementary Teacher/Babson Park Elementary School

Lorrie Driggers Phillips
M.A., Curriculum and Instruction; B.A., Early Childhood and Elementary Education; Elementary Teacher/Babson Park Elementary School

Lost Classics
Book Company
Lake Wales, Florida

PUBLISHER'S NOTE

Recognizing the need to return to more traditional principles in education, Lost Classics Book Company is republishing forgotten late 19th and early 20th century literature and textbooks to aid parents in the education of their children.

The Elson Readers—Book Two, which this volume is meant to accompany, has been assigned a reading level of 500L. More information concerning this reading level assessment may be attained by visiting www.lexile.com.

The Authors

Cynthia Keel Landen graduated with degrees in early childhood and elementary education from the University of Florida. She earned her master's degree in educational leadership at the University of South Florida. She is an elementary teacher with eighteen years of experience and is currently teaching fifth grade at Babson Park Elementary School in Babson Park, Florida.

Lorrie Driggers Phillips graduated from Florida Southern College with degrees in early childhood and elementary education. She received her master's degree in curriculum and instruction from the University of Southern Mississippi. She taught for thirteen years.

© Copyright 2005
Lost Classics Book Company
ISBN 978-1-890623-26-5
Designed to Accompany
The Elson Readers—Book Two
ISBN 978-1-890623-16-6
Part of *The Elson Readers*
Nine Volumes: *Primer* through *Book Eight*
ISBN 978-1-890623-23-4

On the Cover:
The Dog in the Manger from Aesop's Fables, pub. by Raphael Tuck & Sons Ltd., London (book illustration) by John Edwin Noble
Private Collection/Bridgeman Art Library
Lost Classics Book Company would also like to thank Lewis Noble, grandson of John Edwin Noble, for his kind assistance.

TABLE OF CONTENTS

3

THE ELSON READERS—BOOK TWO
A TEACHER'S GUIDE

FOREWORD

Preparing your child for reading and writing is a delicate process. All children move through the developmental stages at different paces. Children need many positive experiences leading them on the path of learning how to read.

The following suggestions are ways for you to help move your child through these stages: keep a vocabulary journal in a notebook, provide daily opportunities for drawing and writing, and read to your child, or have him or her read independently daily.

Always have lined and unlined paper and many writing tools on hand for your child. Children need to have their fine motor skills exercised by having many opportunities to draw and write. Research topics of interest by using the library or the computer to show the different methods of finding new information. Turn the new found information into a writing project.

Research shows that reading to your child is the best way to promote successful reading. For the greatest results, read to your child daily. Let your child pick the books or stories you read together. Take turns reading the selected books. Your child can understand something that is two years above his or her own reading level.

The Elson Readers—Book Two
A Teacher's Guide

How to Use This Book

The Elson Readers, Book Two is filled with enjoyable selections for your child to learn from and enjoy. The book is organized in the following themes: Children, Fables, Animals, Birds, Folk Tales, Seasons and Festivals, Flowers, and Fairies and Fairy Tales.

You could start collecting pictures, books, magazines, posters, cards, stuffed animals, puzzles, puppets, and other educational items to go with these themes. These items can to be used as learning tools to enhance the stories in this book.

If your child is ready for *Book Two,* he or she is continuing to progress in his or her reading and writing skills. He or she has had many successes in these areas and is now ready to build on his or her skills. Lists of words will be provided for each story. Some of the vocabulary words are words that are related to the story and probably will not be found in a dictionary. Some examples are: Top-knot, squee-hee-hee, and summer-maker. Use clues from the selection to figure out the intended meaning of words such as these. We suggest that your child learn these words prior to reading the stories. One way of teaching the words is for your child to write one word at the top of a page in the vocabulary journal. Your child can then use the word correctly in a sentence and may even draw a picture that illustrates the word. Another method for learning and reviewing the vocabulary words is by using index cards. The words can go on one side of the card and the sentences or pictures on the other. These cards are great for reviewing all the words.

Your child is starting to comprehend the text better due to age appropriate abilities. You will find comprehension questions for most of the stories. The questions will be written in one of three formats. The formats include: literal, implied, vocabulary, and creative. Literal questions are answered right in the story. An example of a literal question is: What is the main character's name? Implied questions are not literally written in the text. Clues and background knowledge are used to answer questions such as: What season is it in this story? Children will look at the pictures and see, for example, children wearing long sleeves and raking the yard and infer the time of the year is fall. Vocabulary questions refer to the words selected for each story. Your child will be asked to give the meaning of the word or use the word in a sentence. Creative questions are where children can dream and be unique. This provides a great opportunity for children to tell, draw, or write about their creations. They may be asked to take the part of a main character and give their reaction to a story event, or they may be asked to come up with a new ending for the story. At this stage of development, students should be able to answer these questions on paper and in complete sentences. Your guidance may be needed at first. If your child is not ready for the written response, he or she may give you the answers orally. Use the answers provided as a guide on how to answer the comprehension questions. Phonics lessons and language skills are provided for each selection. Answers will also be provided

A NOTE ABOUT THIS GUIDE

Teachers and students alike may notice a difference in punctuation, capitalization, and spelling between the prose and poetry sections in the reader. Rules for these matters have changed since the original reader's publication, and we have decided that in the prose sections it would be in the best interest of the student to update these items so they will learn these rules as practiced today. However, the stories remain completely unabridged. We have exercised constraint, and typical changes consist of, for example: commas used in place of semicolons when appropriate, lowercase treatment of words not personified, or hyphenated spelling of words being contracted to modern spellings. We have, however, followed the traditional editorial practice of not changing these items in works of poetry, leaving these matters to the prerogative of the poet.

We have used *The Chicago Manual of Style,* 14th Edition, published by the University of Chicago, as our primary reference for these changes.

Objectives—

By completing *Book Two,* the following objectives will be met:

1. The student will predict what a story is about based on its title and illustrations.
2. The student will identify words and construct meaning from text, illustrations, use of phonics, and context clues.
3. The student will use knowledge of developmental-level vocabulary in reading.
4. The student will increase comprehension by retelling and discussion.
5. The student will determine the main idea and supporting details from text.
6. The student will use simple reference materials to obtain information.
7. The student will show an awareness of a beginning, middle, and end in passages.
8. The student will follow simple sets of instructions for simple tasks using logical sequencing of steps.
9. The student will listen for a variety of purposes, including curiosity, pleasure, getting directions, performing tasks, solving problems, and following rules.
10. The student will retell details of information heard, including sequence of events.
11. The student will determine the main idea through illustrations.
12. The student will recognize basic patterns in and functions of language.
13. The student will understand that word choice can shape ideas, feelings, and actions.
14. The student will identify and use repetition, rhyme, and rhythm in oral and written text.
15. The student will identify the story elements of setting, plot, character, problem, and solution.

THE WAKE-UP STORY, p. 9

Preteach the following vocabulary: ready, path, pump, nice, clear, bath, woodpile, chips, cook, rich, Top-knot, Biddy, scratching, new-laid, bathed, dressed, and while.

Answer the following comprehension questions on paper.

Literal

1. What were the animals waiting for at the beginning of the story? The animals were waiting for Baby Ray to wake up and come to the window.

Implied

2. Was the setting of this story in the past, present, or future? Give reasons for your answer. This story took place in the past because Baby Ray's mother had to get water from a pump and heat the water with wood chips.

Implied

3. Why do you think there was a path along the garden to the old pump? There was probably a path along the garden to the old pump because Mother had to get water often, and she went the same way each time.

Literal

4. After Mother collected the water and wood chips, who did she visit next and for what reason? After Mother collected the water and wood chips, she visited the cow to get milk for Baby Ray.

Literal

5. What did Top-Knot Biddy agree to give Mother for Baby Ray? Top-Knot Biddy agreed to give Mother a new-laid egg for Baby Ray.

Literal

6. What did Mother want from the tree? Mother wanted a pretty, red apple from the tree.

Vocabulary

7. What is a wood chip? A wood chip is a small piece of wood.

Implied

8. What do you think Mother will do with the water, wood

chips, milk, egg, and apple? Mother will use the water, wood chips, milk, egg, and apple to make Baby Ray breakfast.

Implied

9. How did Mother know the "Wake-Up" story? Mother knew the "Wake-Up" story because the happenings in the story were what Mother did before Baby Ray woke up.

Creative

10. You read about how Baby Ray starts his day. Tell about how you start your day. (Accept reasonable answers.)

The phonics lesson is a focus on long *a*. Words with a long *a* sound are words like: *game, rain,* and *same*. Have your child make a list of the words from the story with the long *a* sound. Some words to be listed are: *baby, Ray, wake, waiting, came, gave,* and *laid*.

The comprehension skill is a sequencing worksheet to order Mother's morning events.

Answers: 1. old pump 2. woodpile 3. cow 4. Top-knot Biddy 5. tree (The answers at the end of each lesson are to the worksheet exercises following each lesson.)

THE WAKE-UP STORY, p. 9

**Sequence the following story events. Cut the boxes apart and glue them
   in the correct order.**

1. _____

2. _____

3. _____

4. _____

5. _____

A. Top-knot Biddy gave an egg new and white.

B. Woodpile gave big, white chips to warm his bath and cook his food.

C. Cow gave warm, rich milk.

D. The old pump gave nice, clear water for the baby's bath.

E. The tree gave an apple, so round and so red.

THE STAR DIPPER, p. 16

Preteach the following vocabulary: dipper, thirsty, tin, dry, sharp, stones, among, started, poured, hand, queer, happened, shining, silver, drink, shone, feel, sparkling, diamonds, ago, shows, and brave.

Answer the following comprehension questions on paper.

Literal

1. Where did the little girl and her mother live? The little girl and her mother lived in a little house near the woods.

Implied

2. Why couldn't the little girl's mother get herself some water? The little girl's mother couldn't get herself some water because she was sick.

Literal

3. Why couldn't the little girl get water for her mother at the pump? The little girl couldn't get water for her mother at the pump because the well was dry.

Literal

4. Why did the little girl think the dog must be thirsty? The little girl thought the dog must be thirsty because all the brooks were dry.

Vocabulary

5. What is another word for brook? Another word for brook is stream.

Implied

6. In the story, the well and the brooks were dry. What does that tell you about the weather? Because the well and brooks were dry, it means there had been no rain for a long time.

Literal

7. What happened to the dipper when the girl gave the old man a drink? When the girl gave the old man a drink, the dipper turned to shining gold.

Implied

8. How did the dipper help the little girl? The dipper helped the girl by turning to silver and then to gold to light the way home.

Implied

9. What is the purpose of this story? The purpose of the story is to explain how the Big Dipper came to be.

Creative

10. Tell how you would react if you had a tin cup that turned silver, then gold, and then into diamonds. (Accept reasonable answers.)

In this tale, we learn about a star dipper in the sky and how it came to be. For a creative extension, have your child choose an object in the sky and make up a tale about how it came to be. Accept reasonable and creative answers.

This old tale contains the words *sky* and *dry*. These are times when *y* is a vowel. See if your child can name other words where *y* is the only vowel. Use the skill sheet for a review of the vowels and when *y* is a vowel.

Possible answers: sky, dry, try, why, by, my, gym, pry, and cry

THE STAR DIPPER, P. 16

A vowel is a sound of speech made by voicing the flow of breath inside the mouth. The vowels are: *a, e, i, o,* and *u.* Words like *sky* and *dry* do not have a vowel, but the *y* acts as the vowel because it has a vowel sound. See if you can think of other words where *y* is a vowel.

_____   _____

_____   _____

_____   _____

_____   _____

Twinkle, Twinkle, Little Star, p. 20

Preteach and review vocabulary: twinkle, blazing, set, dew, often, traveler, and though.

There are no comprehension questions for this poem.

This poem allows a great opportunity to research facts about stars. Refer to the poem for guidance in helping your child form questions to research. For example, find out what makes the star look like a diamond in the sky. Another example is questioning if a star is gone when the sun is in the sky. You may then want to make a chart comparing statements from the poem about stars to the facts you found out about stars.

The poem is organized in verses of 4 lines. Be creative, follow the rhyming pattern, and make up a verse on your own using the provided worksheet.

Answer: Accept creative poetry writing.

TWINKLE, TWINKLE, LITTLE STAR P. 20

**Write your own verse to the poem. Be sure to follow the rhyming pattern
and make the first two lines rhyme and the last two lines rhyme.**

_____

_____

_____

_____

WHAT LIGHTS THE STARS?, p. 21

Preteach and review vocabulary: half, band, danced, a-searching, skies, minute, and course.

There are no comprehension questions for this poem.

At the end of the poem is a question. Your child can use the facts found in the research of stars from the previous poem to answer that question. Have your child write his or her response in the form of a paragraph.

The vowel sound is long *i*. Use the provided worksheet to practice this skill.

Answers: *igh* – lights, night, right, bright, lighted
Other spellings – I've, times, I, skies, fireflies

WHAT LIGHTS THE STARS?, P. 21

This poem contains many words with the long *i* sound. In some of the words, igh is used to make the long *i* sound. Find the 5 words that use the *igh* spelling and 5 other words from the poem with the long *i* sound.

igh   other spellings

_____   _____

_____   _____

_____   _____

_____   _____

_____   _____

THE NAUGHTY SHADOW, P. 22

Preteach and review vocabulary: naughty, stood, toward, and oho.

Answer the following comprehension questions.

Literal

1. What did the little boy in this story want? The little boy in the story wanted his shadow to come to him.

Implied

2. Why didn't the shadow go to the boy? The shadow did not go to the boy because shadows can't move by themselves. A shadow can only move when the light changes or an object moves.

Vocabulary

3. Use the word naughty in a sentence. (Accept reasonable answers.)

Implied

4. How old was the little boy in this story? The little boy was probably four or five because he was old enough to play outside by himself, yet he was too young to understand how a shadow works.

Creative

5. What do you think the boy will do now that he knows how to get his shadow to come to him? (Accept reasonable answers.)

This tale has some long *e* words such as *me* and *please*. Make a list of other long *e* words with the *e* spelling and the *ea* spelling. Your child can start by making rhyming words to the given words.

The worksheet is a practice in using the past tense of verbs.

Answers: 1. wanted 2. want 3. turn 4. turned 5. looked 6. look

THE NAUGHTY SHADOW, P. 22

A verb is an action word. Sometimes we tell about something that has happened in the past. Usually the *ed* ending is used to show the past tense of verbs. Choose the correct form of verb to go in each sentence.

1. The little boy _____ his shadow to come to him. (want, wanted)

2. I _____ you to come to me now. (want, wanted)

3. He will _____ and walk away. (turn, turned)

4. The shadow _____ when the little boy did. (turn, turned)

5. The little boy _____ and saw the shadow following him. (look, looked)

6. If you will _____, you will see your shadow, too. (look, looked).

MY SHADOW, P. 24

Preteach and review the following vocabulary: goes, use, heels, funniest, proper, which, shoots, India-rubber ball, none, buttercup, lazy, and arrant.

There are no comprehension questions for this poem.

This poem has lots of long *e* words. Some have the *ee* spelling. Add to your long *e* list you made from the previous poem. Be sure to make a column for the *ee* spelling.

Use the following worksheet to practice skills in inferencing, which is using clues from the selection to answer implied questions.

Answers:

1. The shadow is like the boy, because the boy's body shades the light to cause the shadow. When the boy moves, the shadow moves.

2. The shadow jumped into bed before the boy, because the light must have been coming from behind the boy, casting the shadow in front of him.

3. The shadow changes sizes because of where the light is coming from.

4. The shadow wasn't out before the sun was up, because there was not enough light to form a shadow.

MY SHADOW, P. 24

Use clues from the poem to answer the following implied questions. This is a skill in inferencing. Be sure to give reasons for your answers.

1. Why is the shadow like the boy from the heels up to the head?

2. Why does the shadow jump into bed before the boy?

3. Why is the shadow sometimes tall and sometimes little?

4. Why wasn't the shadow around before the sun was up?

BED IN SUMMER, p. 26

Preteach and review the following vocabulary: candle, quite, grown-up, past, seem, and hard.

There are no comprehension questions for this poem.

This poem provides a great opportunity to review the long vowel sounds of *a, e,* and *i.* Have your child find the words from the poem with these sounds and put them on a chart.

The skill is on opposites. Use the provided worksheet for practice.

Answers: 1. down 2. day 3. dark 4. night 5. off 6. stop 7. easy or soft 8. out 9. work 10. cloudy

BED IN SUMMER, P. 26

Opposites are words like *hot* and *cold*. Give the word that means the opposite of the word given.

1. up   _____

2. night   _____

3. light   _____

4. day   _____

5. on   _____

6. go   _____

7. hard   _____

8. in   _____

9. play   _____

10. clear   _____

LUCKY HANS, p. 27

Preteach and review the following vocabulary: lucky, been, pay, piece, shoulder, hot, heavy, riding, rode, foot, load, trade, reins, driving, brought, sunny, clapped, drove, drop, kicked, dust, butcher, wheelbarrow, killed, beef, pork, troubles, carrying, stolen, thief, throw, rid, scissors-grinder, pocket, either, answered, done, need, grindstone, bank, stooped, and watched.

Answer the following comprehension questions on paper.

Literal

1. How long had Hans been working for his master? Hans had worked for his master for seven years.

Literal

2. Why did the master give Hans a large piece of silver? The master gave Hans a large piece of silver because Hans had worked hard.

Implied

3. Why did Hans work such a long time far away from his mother? Hans probably worked such a long time and far away from his mother because she could not support Hans. Possibly Hans was learning a trade so he could support himself.

Literal

4. For what did Hans trade the piece of silver? Hans traded the piece of silver for a fine horse.

Implied

5. Why did Hans fall off the horse? Hans probably fell off the horse because he was going too fast, and Hans was not an experienced rider.

Implied

6. What does the author mean in the story when it says, "Hans drove the cow"? The author meant that Hans walked beside or behind the cow and prodded her along.

Vocabulary

7. Tell about a time when you were cross. (Accept reasonable answers.)

Literal

8. Why did Hans trade the pig for a goose? Hans traded the

pig for a goose because a pig in the next town had been stolen, and Hans did not want the people to think that he was the thief.

Implied

9. Why did Hans feel lucky when the grindstone fell into the pond? Hans felt lucky when the grindstone fell into the pond, because that meant he would not have to carry the heavy grindstone.

Creative

10. Do you think Hans really is lucky? Tell why or why not. (Accept reasonable answers.)

Irregular past tense verbs are words that do not have *ed* endings. Use the provided worksheet to practice this skill.

The phonics skill is the *tr* blend from the words *trade, tried,* and *troubles.* Have your child brainstorm more words with the *tr* blend.

For an extension, have your child give the cause-effect relationship of each of Lucky Hans's trades. For example: Hans traded the silver for the horse because it got heavy.

Answers: 1. sang 2. rang 3. heard 4. bought 5. found 6. drank 7. fell 8. took

LUCKY HANS, p. 27

You learned about how you add an *ed* to some verbs to make them past tense. Verbs in which you do not add the *ed* ending are called irregular verbs. The past tense form of drive is drove and ride is rode. Write the irregular past tense verb next to the present tense verb.

1. sing _____

2. ring _____

3. hear _____

4. buy _____

5. find _____

6. drink _____

7. fall _____

8. take _____

THE LOST DOLL, p. 38

Preteach and review the following vocabulary: charmingly, curled, heath, week, folks, terribly, changed, paint, washed, arm's, trodden, least, and sake.

There are no comprehension questions for this poem.

In the poem, the little girl's doll was lost for more than a week and was found in poor condition. Have your child write about the problems the doll probably experienced during the week she was lost.

The phonic skill is the *ch* blend from the words *cheeks* and *charming*. Use the practice sheet for this skill.

Possible answers: chair, church, chick, chip, chirp, charcoal, chalk, chain, chest, chicken, etc.

THE LOST DOLL, P. 38

The poem has two words that begin with the *ch* blend. Think of ten other words that begin in the same way. Choose three words to illustrate at the bottom.

1. _____   2. _____

3. _____   4. _____

5. _____   6. _____

7. _____   8. _____

9. _____   10. _____

THE ANT AND THE GRASSHOPPER, p. 40

Preteach and review the following vocabulary: grasshopper, same, worker, harm, and stiff.

Answer the following comprehension questions on paper.

Literal

1. What was the difference between the ant and the grasshopper? The difference between the ant and the grasshopper was the ant was hard working while the grasshopper was lazy.

Literal

2. When winter came, what happened to the ant? When winter came, the ant had a warm house full of food.

Literal

3. What happened to the grasshopper when winter came? When winter came, the grasshopper was very cold and had nothing to eat.

Implied

4. What did ant mean when she said, "Now you may dance for your supper"? When ant told grasshopper to dance for his supper, she meant that he could dance for her and she would give him food.

Creative

5. If you were the ant, what would you do when the grasshopper asked for food? Why? (Accept any reasonable answers.)

This story contains many short *a* words. Have your child complete the following worksheet to practice this skill.

Answers: 1. ant 2. angry 3. sad 4. dance 5. last 6. dad 7. grass 8. sang 9. have 10. harm

THE ANT AND THE GRASSHOPPER, P. 40

Fill in the blanks with the matching short *a* words from the word list.

ant, grass, dance, harm, last, have, dad, sad, angry, sang

1. **A small insect:** _____

2. **Really mad:** _____

3. **Not happy:** _____

4. **Move your body:** _____

5. **Opposite of first:** _____

6. **A parent:** _____

7. **Gets mowed:** _____

8. **Form of sing:** _____

9. **To hold or own:** _____

10. **To hurt or damage:** _____

THE FOOLISH FROG, p. 42

Preteach and review the following vocabulary: frog, ox, animal, herself, strange, young, burst, and silly.

Answer the following comprehension questions on paper.

Literal

1. Why were the little frogs frightened? The little frogs were frightened because they saw an ox, and they had never seen one before.

Implied

2. Why did Mother Frog keep trying to puff herself up? Mother frog kept trying to puff herself up so she would be as big as the ox. She was proud and did not want the ox to be bigger than her.

Vocabulary

3. Explain how the word *beast* is used in this story. The word beast is used to describe a four-footed animal. In this story, the beast was the ox.

Literal

4. What finally happens to Mother Frog as she puffs herself up? As Mother Frog puffs herself up, she finally puffs so hard that she bursts.

Implied

5. What is the moral of this story? The moral of the story is that it is foolish to try to do something that is impossible.

This story has several short *o* words. Use the provided worksheet to practice this skill.

Possible Answers:
box, fox, rocks, socks
bond, fond
gout, pout, about
hour, sour, tower, flower, power
robot, dot, hot, lot, pot, rot, tot

THE FOOLISH FROG, p. 42

Listed here are five short *o* words from the story. List two more words
that rhyme with the given word. All of the words will have a short
o sound. Then choose three words to write and illustrate at the
bottom.

Ox   _____   _____

Pond   _____   _____

Out   _____   _____

Our   _____   _____

Not   _____   _____

PLEASING EVERYBODY, p. 44

Preteach and review the following vocabulary: pleasing, everybody, taking, donkey, easier, ashamed, women, selfish, room, enough, able, pole, carried, untied, drive, and nobody.

Answer the following comprehension questions on paper.

Literal

1. Why were the old man and little boy taking the donkey to the next town? The old man and the little boy were taking the donkey to the next town because they wanted to sell it.

Implied

2. Why did the old man keep listening to everyone about who should ride the donkey? The old man kept listening to everyone about who should ride the donkey because he was trying to please everyone.

Literal

3. How were the old man and the little boy able to carry the donkey? The old man and little boy were able to carry the donkey by tying the donkey's legs to a pole and carrying it over their shoulders.

Implied

4. What lesson did the old man probably learn? The old man probably learned that it is better to do what you think is best instead of listening to lots of other people.

Creative

5. Tell how it could be unwise or dangerous to try to please everyone. (Accept reasonable answers.)

We know from the story that the boy and his father did not succeed in pleasing everybody. If you could have retold this story, how would you have changed it? Rewrite the story in your own words to show how success could have been possible.

For the phonics skill use the following worksheet on the *th* blend.

Answers: thanks, Thursday, think, third, thirsty, theater, thin, thermometer, thorn, thief

PLEASING EVERYBODY, p. 44

This story contains some words that begin with a *th* blend, such as *they, them, that, their, think,* and *the*. Fill in the blanks with the rest of the word to match the given description.

Th_____   This is what you say after someone hands you something.

Th_____   This is the fifth day of the week.

Th_____   This is what you do with your brain.

Th_____   This is not first or second.

Th_____   This is when you want water to drink.

Th_____   This is where you see a movie.

Th_____   This is the same as skinny.

Th_____   This is what is used to check for a fever.

Th_____   This hurts if it gets stuck in your foot.

Th_____   This is a person who steals from others.

THE DOG IN THE MANGER, P. 47

Preteach and review the following vocabulary: manger, ought, starve, life, and else.

There are no comprehension questions for this fable.

Let your child tell you a tale of a time when someone was acting selfish to them like the dog is acting to the ox.

Use the provided worksheet to review the long and short vowel sounds of *a*. Remember; the long *a* sound says the sound of *a*, as in tr*a*de.

Answers:

long *a*: manger, lay, hay, came, made

short *a*: that, was, wanted, barked, have, any, said, starve, cannot

THE DOG IN THE MANGER, p. 47

Fill in the chart with the correct words to match each vowel sound. You may write the words in or cut and paste them in place.

long *a*	short *a*

manger	lay	that	was	hay	came

wanted	barked	have	any	said	made	starve	cannot

LITTLE MOUSE AND THE STRANGERS, p. 48

Preteach and review the following vocabulary: strangers, fur, mine, quick, gentle, speak, sound, purr-r, danger, dreadful, most, listen, chin, moved, wild, stretched, squee-hee-hee, mind, fierce, remember, and deeds.

Answer the following comprehension questions on paper.

Literal

1. Why did Little Mouse go out to see the world? Little Mouse went out to see the world because she was tired of their little home.

Implied

2. Had Little Mouse asked Mother's permission to go to the barnyard? How do you know? No, Little Mouse had not asked her mother's permission to go to the barnyard because Mother Mouse asked Little Mouse where she had been.

Literal

3. What two animals did Little Mouse meet in the barnyard? Little Mouse met a cat and a cock when she went into the barnyard.

Implied

4. Explain what Mother Mouse meant when she told Little Mouse "that good deeds are better than good looks." When Mother Mouse told Little Mouse that good deeds are better than good looks, she meant that the way someone acts is a better way to judge their character than the way they look.

Creative

5. Pretend you are Little Mouse and describe another animal you saw in the barnyard. (Example: I saw a beautiful animal with fur like mine. He had long hair on his neck and four long legs.)

This story contains many words that imitate sounds. This kind of word is called an *onomatopoeia*. Some examples of onomatopoeia words are: squeak, purr-r, squee-hee-hee, and cock-a-doodle-doo. Brainstorm with your child more words that fit this classification. Use the following worksheet to write the words and draw illustrations to go with them.

Possible Answers: ding-a-ling (bell), mooo (cow), pop (balloon or bubble), hiss (snake), buzz (bee)

LITTLE MOUSE AND THE STRANGERS, p. 48

Onomatopoeia words are words that imitate the sound it represents. Think of more words that fit this description. Write the word and illustrate it in the box provided.

THE COW, P. 53

Preteach and review the following vocabulary: cream, apple-tart, wanders, lowing, stray, blown, pass, and showers.

There are no comprehension questions for this poem.

This poem is designed with alternating pairs of rhyming words. Have your child point out the rhyming words in the poem.

There are words in the poem that contain the consonant plus *l* blends. List more words on the worksheet in each category.

Answers: Accept words with the correct blends.

THE COW, P. 53

This poem has the words *flowers, pleasant,* and *blown*. Think of other words with the same blend to add to the chart.

fl	pl	bl
_____	_____	_____
_____	_____	_____
_____	_____	_____
_____	_____	_____
_____	_____	_____
_____	_____	_____
_____	_____	_____
_____	_____	_____
_____	_____	_____

TARO AND THE TURTLE, p. 54

Preteach and review the following vocabulary: Taro, turtle, fisherman, teased, teasing, stroked, thousand, boat, saving, sea king's, palace, bottom, bloomed, gatekeeper, helpers, princess, yesterday, saved, and share.

Answer the following comprehension questions on paper.

Literal

1. What job did Taro have? Taro was a fisherman.

Implied

2. Was Taro good at his job? Why or why not? Taro was very good at his job, because he could catch more fish than anyone else.

Literal

3. What did Taro see on his way home? On his way home, Taro saw some boys who had caught a turtle and were teasing it.

Implied

4. Why did Taro give money to the boys? Taro gave money to the boys so they would give Taro the turtle. Then Taro took the turtle to the sea and let it go.

Literal

5. Why was the turtle calling Taro? The turtle was calling Taro because she wanted to thank Taro for saving her life.

Literal

6. Where did the turtle want to take Taro? The turtle wanted to take Taro to the sea king's palace at the bottom of the sea.

Vocabulary

7. What is a gatekeeper? A gatekeeper is the person in charge of opening and closing the gate.

Implied

8. What surprise does Taro get when he visits the sea king's palace? Taro is surprised to find that the turtle he saved is really the sea king's child.

Implied

9. How does the sea king's child reward Taro? The sea king's child rewards Taro by inviting him to live with her. She said she would share everything with Taro, and they would live 1,000 years in the land of summer under the sea.

Implied

10. Do you think this story is fiction or nonfiction? Give two reasons for your answer. This story is fiction because turtles can't talk, turtles can't suddenly grow very large, birds can't sing, and flowers can't bloom underwater, and Taro would not be able to breathe underwater. (Accept other reasonable answers.)

On the worksheet, your child will draw an illustration from the beginning, middle, and end of the story.

Answers: Accept reasonable answers.

TARO AND THE TURTLE, P. 54

Beginning

Middle

End

The Elephant and the Monkey, p. 59

Preteach and review the following vocabulary: elephant, monkey, quarrel, climb, agree, pick, trunk, stream, neither, strength, quickness, and gathered.

Answer the following comprehension questions on paper.

Vocabulary

1. What is a quarrel? A quarrel is an argument or a fight.

Literal

2. Why were the elephant and the monkey quarreling? The elephant and monkey were quarreling about which was better between being strong or being quick.

Implied

3. Why do you think the elephant and the monkey went to the owl for advice? The elephant and the monkey probably went to the owl for advice because owls are supposed to be wise.

Literal

4. What did the owl tell the elephant and the monkey to do? The owl told the elephant and the monkey to cross the river, pick some fruit, and bring it back to him.

Vocabulary

5. Use the word *swift* in a sentence. (Accept any reasonable answers.)

Implied

6. Why do you think a monkey would be afraid of a swift river? A monkey would be afraid of drowning in a swift river. Monkeys are light, and the current of the river would be strong enough to keep a monkey from getting to shore.

Literal

7. Why could the elephant not get the fruit by himself? The elephant could not get the fruit by himself because the fruit was too high in the tree, and the tree was too strong to knock down.

Literal

8. How was the monkey able to get the fruit? The monkey was able to get the fruit because he could climb.

Implied

9. Why did the owl give this task to the elephant and monkey instead of another task? Owl gave the elephant and the monkey

this task instead of another, because he wanted the elephant and the monkey to have to work together to complete the job.

Creative

10. Tell about a time when you had to work as a team to get a job or task done. (Accept reasonable answers.)

This story has many short *u* words. Use the worksheet to practice this skill.

Answers: Pull, run, trunk, hungry, us, up, and until should be colored.

THE ELEPHANT AND THE MONKEY, P. 59

Color the boxes that have words with the short *u* sound. The short *u* sound is in the words *upon* and *just*.

pull	up
run	use
trunk	fruit
hungry	until
us	you

THE BEAR WHO PLAYED SOLDIER, p. 62

Preteach and review the following vocabulary: bear, soldier, tame, march, really, inn, upstairs, gun, tramp, snuffed, rat-a-tat-tat, hold, left, and led.

Answer the following comprehension questions on paper.

Literal

1. What was unusual about the bear in this story? The bear in this story was unusual, because he could march, play ball, and dance.

Vocabulary

2. Tell the opposite of tame. The opposite of tame is wild.

Implied

3. How do you think the man in the story earned money? The man in the story earned money by charging people to see his bear march, play ball, and dance.

Literal

4. What were the little boys doing? The little boys were upstairs playing soldier.

Implied

5. How were the little boys related? The three little boys were brothers because they had the same father and mother.

Literal

6. How did the little boys feel when the bear came upstairs? The little boys felt frightened when the bear came upstairs because they hid in the corners of the room.

Implied

7. Why do you think the bear went upstairs? The bear probably went upstairs because he heard the children playing, and he wanted to play too.

Implied

8. Why did the children finally come out of the corners? The children came out of the corners because they thought the bear was a dog, because it was walking around sniffing them.

Literal

9. What did the mother do when she saw the big bear? When the mother saw the big bear, she became frightened and called for help.

Creative

10. What do you think the little boys and the bear did after the mother and the bear's master had found them? (Accept reasonable answers.)

Use the following worksheet to practice the skill of sequencing.

Practice the short *e* sound by playing a game of building words. Use the beginnings: *the, le, ne,* and *ge* to add to in building words with the short *e* sound.

Answers: 1. 32154 2. 21435 3. 31524 4. 24315 5. 31524

THE BEAR WHO PLAYED SOLDIER, P. 62

Use the numbers *1-5* to put the following sets in order.

1. ___ third   2. ___ 8:00 A.M.   3. ___ eat lunch

    ___ then   ___ 2:00 P.M.   ___ wake up

    ___ first   ___ 8:00 A.M.   ___ go to bed

    ___ finally   ___ 12:00 A.M.   ___ brush teeth

    ___ fourth   ___ 2:00 A.M.   ___ do homework

4. ___ hit the ball   5. ___ We pack our suitcases.

    ___ slide into 2nd base   ___ Our family plans a vacation.

    ___ run to 1st base   ___ We leave to go on our trip.

    ___ walk up to the plate   ___ We buy snacks to take on the trip.

    ___ next batter up   ___ Dad packs our things in the car.

THE NEW VOICES, P. 65

Preteach and review the following vocabulary: sparrow, bleat, teach, taught, afterwards, sheepfold, late, tapped, and breakfast.

Answer the following comprehension questions on paper.

Literal

1. What did every bird and every animal want to do? Every bird and every animal wanted to change their voice.

Literal

2. The wise man agreed to teach the birds and animals how to change their voices if they would do what? The wise man agreed to teach the birds and animals how to change their voices if they would make good use of their new voices.

Implied

3. Did the birds and animals use their new voices for a good use? Why or why not? The birds and animals did not use their new voices for a good use because they used their new voices to trick other birds and animals to come close, and then the animals with a new voice ate them.

Implied

4. What time of day does the hawk trick the sparrows? How do you know? It is morning when the hawk tricks the sparrows because the little sparrows think it is their father bringing them breakfast.

Literal

5. What does the wise man tell the birds and animals that they must do at the end of the story? At the end of the story, the wise man tells the birds and animals they must take back their own voices because they did not make good use of them.

Use the provided worksheet to practice the use of quotation marks. Show your child how they are used in the story.

The phonics skill is the short *i* sound found in *chirp, wish,* and *in*. Make a chart listing the long and short *i* words found in this story.

Answers:

1. "I want to go home," said Sam.
2. Mom replied, "The girls are outside playing."

3. Bobby and Andrea yelled, "We want ice cream!"
4. Shelby asked, "Can I go over to my friend's house?"
5. "Could I have some more popcorn?" asked Colt.
6. "Gary, go clean your room," said Mom.

THE NEW VOICES, p. 65

Quotation marks are used to show exactly what a person said or asked. Look at the following examples from your story.

Example: The fox said, "I want to crow like a cock."
Example: "We are all tired of our voices," they said.

Now put the commas and quotation marks in the correct places in the following sentences.

1. I want to go home said Sam.

2. Mom replied The girls are outside playing.

3. Bobby and Andrea yelled We want ice cream!

4. Shelby asked Can I go over to my friend's house?

5. Could I have some more popcorn? asked Colt.

6. Gary, go clean your room said Mom.

THE SWALLOW, p. 68

Preteach and review the following vocabulary: swallow, sun-loving, hurrying, o'er, certain, cloudy, and follow.

There are no comprehension questions for this poem.

This poem tells about the seasons of summer and winter. Have your child make a poster showing the different activities that are enjoyed in each of these seasons. They may draw the pictures or cut them out of magazines.

The word *swallow* begins with the consonant blend of *sw*. Use the worksheet to practice this skill.

Possible answers: swim, swam, swarm, sweat, sweet, sweater, sweep, switch, swatch, swap, swish

THE SWALLOW, P. 68

The *sw* blend is found at the beginning of the word *swallow*. Think of more words with the same consonant blend to put in the boxes. Choose a few to illustrate.

THE OLD WOMAN WHO WANTED ALL THE CAKES, P. 69

Preteach and review the following vocabulary: cakes, baking, word, cape, cap, those, dough, oven, and woodpecker.

Answer the following comprehension questions on paper.

Literal

1. What was the old woman wearing? The old woman was wearing a black dress, a white cape, and a little red cap.

Implied

2. Does this story take place in the past, present, or future? How do you know? This story takes place in the past because women don't wear capes and little caps anymore.

Literal

3. Why did the poor old man want one of the old woman's cakes? The poor old man wanted one of the old woman's cakes because he was hungry.

Implied

4. Each time the old woman made a cake for the poor old man, the cake would grow bigger and bigger and then she would keep it for herself. Why did the old woman do that? The old woman kept the cakes that grew bigger and bigger for herself because she was selfish.

Literal

5. What happened to the old woman when she ate the cakes? When the old woman ate the cakes, she grew smaller and smaller and finally turned into a woodpecker.

Creative

6. Why do you suppose the old woman changed into a woodpecker instead of some other bird? (Accept answers related to the old woman's clothes compared to the colors of a woodpecker.)

In some cases, you can change the vowel sound from a short sound to a long sound by adding an *e* to the end of the word. Use the worksheet for this skill.

In this tale, the old woman's clothes change into feathers. Make up a tale about how a different bird could have come to be.

Answers: 1. cape 2. fate 3. slate 4. tape 5. rate 6. pane 7. hate 8. paste 9. mate 10. bade

THE OLD WOMAN WHO WANTED ALL THE CAKES, P. 69

Change the following short *a* words into long *a* sounds by adding an *e*.
Select one pair of words to illustrate at the bottom of the page.

1. cap _____

2. fat _____

3. slat _____

4. tap _____

5. rat _____

6. pan _____

7. hat _____

8. past _____

9. mat _____

10. bad _____

ROBIN'S SECRET, P. 72

Preteach and review the following vocabulary: secret, cherry, shan't, and whole.

There are no comprehension questions for this poem.

This story has the contraction shan't in it. Use the skill worksheet to practice contractions.

Have your child write a five-step procedure to show sequencing. It can relate to the story or his or her everyday life actions. For example: 1. Mother bird gathers materials for her nest. 2. She keeps her eggs warm by sitting on them. 3. Baby birds hatch. 4. Mother gathers food for the baby birds. 5. Baby birds learn to fly.

Answers: 1. couldn't 2. wouldn't 3. don't 4. I've 5. I'd
Accept reasonable sentences.

ROBIN'S SECRET, p. 72

A contraction is when you have two words joined together. Combine the following sets of words into contractions. Then write a sentence using the contraction.

1. could+not=_____

_____

_____

2. would+not=_____

_____

_____

3. do + not = _____

_____

_____

4. I + have = _____

_____

_____

5. I + would = _____

_____

_____

LITTLE BIRD BLUE, p. 74

Preteach and review the following vocabulary: weather, skates, sleds, honey-bees, hum, pussies, and willow-trees.

There are no comprehension questions for this poem.

There are a few compound words in this poem, such as *snowbanks*, *springtime*, *honey-bees*, and *willow-trees*. Sometimes a hyphen is used to make some compound words. Use the provided worksheet to practice making compound words.

Use the words *sleds, heads, weather,* and *then* to review the short *e* sound.

Your child can write about the signs of spring coming in your neighborhood as a writing extension.

Answers: everything, basketball, playground, plaything, playtime, underground, underwear, treetop, something, sometime, and housework

LITTLE BIRD BLUE, p. 74

Compound words are when two words are joined together to form one word. Use the following sets of words to make compound words.

every	ground
basket	thing
play	ball
under	top
tree	wear
some	work
house	time

_____

_____

_____

_____

_____

_____

_____

_____

_____

THE MAGPIE'S LESSON, p. 75

Preteach and review the following vocabulary: magpie, lesson, mud, shape, thrush, sticks, twigs, wind, lining, suits, lined, and alike.

Answer the following comprehension questions on paper.

Literal

1. Who showed all the other birds how to build a nest? The magpie showed all the other birds how to build a nest.

Implied

2. Why did the thrush fly away after the magpie had only shown the first step? The thrush flew away after only the first step because she thought that was all. She was impatient and wanted to get started on her own nest.

Vocabulary

3. What are twigs? A twig is a small, dry piece of branch.

Implied

4. Why do some of the birds line their nests with soft feathers? Some of the birds line their nests with soft feathers to make the nests warmer.

Implied

5. Why was this story written? This story was written to explain why the nests of birds are not alike.

Use the following skill sheet to practice sequencing.

The phonics skill is a review of the short *u* sound found in the words *mud, cup,* and *thrush*. This would be a time to teach the long *u* sound found in the words *use* and *suits*. Long *u* sounds in words are not as plentiful as other vowel sounds. Have your child think of other long *u* words to list.

Answers: 1. 52413 2. 53124 3. 35124 4. 35214

THE MAGPIE'S LESSON, p. 75

Let's review sequencing. Put the following items in order from first to last. Place a 1 next to the first item, a 2 next to the second and so on. On item number 2, start with 12:00 P.M.

1. ____ November

   ____ March

   ____ July

   ____ February

   ____ May

2. ____ 3:22 A.M.

   ____ 12:00 A.M.

   ____ 12:00 P.M.

   ____ 10:28 P.M.

   ____ 1:30 A.M.

3. ____ You begin walking.

   ____ You start school.

   ____ You are born.

   ____ You drink a bottle.

   ____ You ride a tricycle.

4. ____ You get to the doctor's office.

   ____ The nurse weighs you on the scale.

   ____ Your mom makes an appointment.

   ____ You have a fever and sore throat.

   ____ The nurse calls you back.

THE LITTLE RABBIT WHO WANTED RED WINGS, P. 77

Preteach and review the following vocabulary: porcupine, hog, sitting, tight, and knocked.

Answer the following comprehension questions on paper.

Literal

1. Where did the little white rabbit live? The little white rabbit lived in a warm hole at the foot of an old tree.

Literal

2. How did White Rabbit's mother feel about him always wishing for something? White Rabbit's mother grew very tired of hearing him always wishing for something.

Implied

3. Why did old Mr. Groundhog tell White Rabbit about the Wishing Pond? Old Mr. Groundhog probably told White Rabbit about the Wishing Pond because he knew the rabbit would make a wish to change and then learn being himself is best.

Literal

4. Where did White Rabbit find the Wishing Pond? White Rabbit found the Wishing Pond in the cool, green woods.

Vocabulary

5. Define the word *queer*. Queer means something that is strange or odd.

Implied

6. Why do you think White Rabbit wished for wings like the little red bird? White Rabbit probably wished for wings like the little red bird because he wanted to try flying.

Literal

7. Why would White Rabbit's mother not let him in that night? White Rabbit's mother would not let him in that night, because she did not know him. She had never seen a rabbit with red wings.

Implied

8. How do you think White Rabbit felt when his mother and all the other animals would not let him come in? White Rabbit probably felt alone and scared when his mother and all the other animals would not let him come in.

Implied

9. Why did Mr. Groundhog recognize White Rabbit when no

one else did? Mr. Groundhog recognized White Rabbit when no one else did, because Mr. Groundhog knew that White Rabbit had visited the Wishing Pond.

Literal

10. How did White Rabbit solve his problem? White Rabbit solved his problem by returning to the Wishing Pond and wishing his wings away.

Adjectives are used frequently in this story. They are used to describe nouns. Use the provided worksheet to write adjectives to go with nouns.

The phonics skill is the *gr* blend found in *groundhog* and *green*. List other words that begin with the same consonant blend.

As a writing extension, have your child write about what they would wish for if they only had one wish.

Answers: Accept reasonable adjectives.

THE LITTLE RABBIT WHO WANTED RED WINGS, p. 77

This story uses many adjectives. Adjectives are words that describe nouns. Examples are *blue*, *sparkly*, and *little*. Fill in each blank with an adjective that describes the noun.

1. a(n) _____ bicycle

2. the _____ girl

3. the _____ boy

4. a(n) _____ sky

5. the _____ door

6. the _____ family

7. the _____ home

8. a(n) _____ cat

9. a(n) _____ turtle

10. a(n) _____, _____ pond

THE ANIMALS THAT FOUND A HOME, p. 81

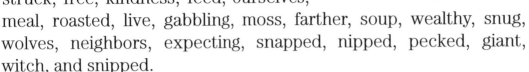

Preteach and review the following vocabulary: ram, fed, mutton, against, struck, free, kindness, feed, ourselves, meal, roasted, live, gabbling, moss, farther, soup, wealthy, snug, wolves, neighbors, expecting, snapped, nipped, pecked, giant, witch, and snipped.

Answer the following comprehension questions on paper.

Implied

1. What is the setting at the beginning of the story? How do you know? The setting at the beginning of the story is on a farm, because there are farm animals, and they are being raised for meat.

Literal

2. Why did the man want the ram to get fat? The man wanted the ram to get fat because he was going to turn the ram into mutton.

Vocabulary

3. What is mutton? Mutton is the name used for sheep meat.

Literal

4. How did the ram escape? The ram escaped by putting his head down and running against the door. He hit the door with his horns, and the door flew open.

Literal

5. What other characters left with the ram? The other characters who left with the ram were the pig, goose, and rooster.

Implied

6. Why did the animals go to the woods to build a house? The animals went to the woods to build the house so the man would not find them.

Implied

7. Why did one of the hungry wolves go to visit his new neighbors? One of the hungry wolves went to visit his new neighbors because he was hoping to get some breakfast.

Literal

8. How did the animals react to the wolf's visit? The animals reacted by attacking the wolf. They were expecting him to come over.

Implied

9. How did the wolves feel about their new neighbors after the wolf's visit? After the wolf's visit, the wolves were afraid of their new neighbors because they kept away from their new neighbors.

Creative

10. Did the wolf who did not come to visit really believe that a giant, troll, and witch were in the house instead of the animals? Why or why not? (Accept reasonable answers.)

Most stories have a problem and a solution. On the worksheet provided, write about the problem and solution in this story.

The phonics skill is the *thr* blend found in the words *threw* and *throw*. Brainstorm more *thr* words.

Answers:

The problem in the story is that the animals were told to eat and get fat for meat.

The solution is that they escaped the farm together and made their own home.

THE ANIMALS THAT FOUND A HOME, P. 81

This story, like most other stories, has a problem and a solution. In your own words, write the problem and solution for this story. At the bottom, draw what you think the inside of the animals' house looked like.

The problem in the story is _____

_____

_____.

The solution is _____

_____

_____.

THE BELL OF ATRI, P. 89

Preteach and review the following vocabulary: Atri, wrong, tower, bell, rope, ring, judges, punish, rang, robes, rung, thin, ding-dong, nap, lame, almost, blind, starving, belongs, castle, war, wherever, unless, bad, shame, word, and stable.

Answer the following comprehension questions on paper.

Literal

1. Who built a tower with a bell in it? Good King John built a tower with a bell in it.

Literal

2. Why was the bell tower built? The bell tower was built so that when someone was in trouble, he or she could ring the bell. When the bell was rung, a judge would come to help.

Implied

3. Why did the king choose a judge to listen to the person who rang the bell? The king probably chose a judge to listen to the person who rang the bell because judges are supposed to be fair and wise.

Literal

4. Why was the horse ringing the bell? The horse was ringing the bell because there was a piece of hay tied around the rope, and the horse was eating the hay making the bell ring.

Literal

5. Why was the judge angry at first? The judge was angry at first because the bell woke him from his nap, and he came to help the person who was in trouble. It turned out to be only a horse.

Implied

6. Why did the judge stop being angry? The judge stopped being angry because he realized that the horse was in trouble.

Vocabulary

7. Use lame in a sentence. (Accept reasonable sentences.)

Implied

8. Why did the horse's master turn the horse out when he got too old to work? The horse's master turned the horse out when he got too old to work because the master did not want to spend money to take care of an old horse.

Implied

9. Why did the judge tell the master he must take care of the horse for the rest of the horse's life? The judge told the master he must take care of the horse for the rest of the horse's life because the horse had worked hard for the master and saved his life many times when he was younger.

Creative

10. Do you think the master took care of the horse for the rest of the horse's life? Why or why not? (Accept reasonable answers.)

The phonics skill is the *br* blend from the words *brave, bring,* and *brought*. Find other words from a previous story with the *br* blend.

Use the worksheet to practice the parts of speech terms: nouns, verbs, and adjectives.

Answers: 1. pops 2. slithers 3. flies 4. laughs 5. buzz 6. hiccups 7. slapped 8. practice

THE BELL OF ATRI, P. 89

A noun is a person, place, thing, or idea. An adjective is a word that describes a noun. A verb shows action. It tells us what a noun does. Example: The pesky ants nibbled on our picnic lunch. *Pesky* is the adjective, *ants* is the noun, and *nibbled* is the verb.
Look at these sentences below. Put the verb that makes the best sense with each phrase.

slapped   slithers   flies   pops   practice   buzz   laughs   hiccups

1. The red balloon _____.

2. A scary snake _____.

3. The little bird _____.

4. The happy girl _____.

5. The swarm of busy bees _____.

6. The boy drinking the orange soda _____.

7. The hungry mosquito was _____ when it landed on my leg.

8. At recess the sweaty students _____ skipping.

THE SUMMER-MAKER, P. 95

Preteach and review the following vocabulary: summer-maker, season, ice, bare, Ojeeg, Indian, deer, feast, bow, arrow, fingers, numb, use, wigwam, magic, meet, tears, smiled, fond, son, otter, beaver, badger, journey, mountain, touched, jumper, breath, rock, fists, breeze, rushed, melted, sparkled, and since.

Answer the following comprehension questions on paper.

Implied

1. Why was this story written? This story was written to explain why we have summer.

Literal

2. Who are the main characters in the story? The main characters in the story are Ojeeg and his father, Big Hunter.

Implied

3. What was Ojeeg's problem? Ojeeg's problem was that he loved to hunt, but he could not stay out very long because the cold made his hands numb. When his hands got numb, he couldn't use his bow and arrow to bring back food.

Literal

4. What did Ojeeg want his father to do? Ojeeg wanted his father to make summer.

Vocabulary

5. Big Hunter was fond of his son. Explain what fond means. Fond means that Big Hunter loved and cherished his son.

Literal

6. Who helped Big Hunter make summer? Big Hunter's friends Otter, Beaver, and Badger helped Big Hunter make summer.

Implied

7. Why did Big Hunter and his friends go up a high mountain? Big Hunter and his friends went up a high mountain so they could get as close to the sky as possible.

Literal

8. How did Big Hunter make summer come? Big Hunter made summer come by punching a large hole in the sky. Summer came down through the hole.

Implied

9. Why did Ojeeg make a feast for his father and his father's friends? Ojeeg made a feast for Big Hunter and his friends because

he wanted to thank them for making summer.

Creative

10. If you were Big Hunter, how would you make a hole in the sky? (Accept creative answers.)

This story is an Indian legend. Go to your local library or the Internet to see if you can uncover some other Indian legends as an extension.

Use the following worksheet to practice vowel sounds.

Answers:

Long *e* sounds—season, years, feast, leaves, beaver, reach, beat

Short *e* sounds—learn, bear, great, breath, beautiful, sweat, instead

THE SUMMER-MAKER, P. 95

You have already learned that the long *e* sound can be found in words like *meet* and *be*. Sometimes the long *e* spelling is *ea*. Use the following word list to write the words that have a long *e* sound in one column and the short *e* sounds in another column.

sweat   beaver   reach   breath   great   years   feast   learn   leaves
season   beautiful   bear   instead   beat

long *e*	short *e*

THE THREE PIGS, P. 103

Preteach and review the following vocabulary: earn, living, straw, huff, rap, third, bricks, rows, juicy, o'clock, these, fair, churn, bought, except, heat, lid, and visit.

There are no comprehension questions for this story because it is such a familiar story.

For an extension, have your child and some friends perform a puppet show to retell the story. Simple puppets can be made from sketches of the characters attached to wooden craft sticks.

Use the worksheet to practice words with the *kn* spelling.

For an extension, compare and contrast this story with *The True Story of the Three Little Pigs* by Jon Scieszka.

Answers: Accept reasonable sentences and illustrations.

THE THREE PIGS, P. 103

The blend *kn* is special because the *k* is silent. Practice saying the following words while pointing to each one. After you have practiced pronouncing these words, choose four to illustrate in the boxes below. Write a sentence for each choice.

knocked   knowledge   knot   know   knit
          knuckle   knight   knee   knife   knew

THE HOUSE IN THE WOODS, P. 111

Preteach and review the following vocabulary: woodcutter, wife, lose, noon, lifted, latch, hearth, speckled, meant, kitchen, dish, stew, large, bump, cellar, sent, tomorrow, hoot, peas, spoke, armful, clean, sheets, ivory, chairs, pinched, center, table, servants, and surprised.

Answer the following comprehension questions on paper.

Literal

1. How many people were in the poor woodcutter's family? There were five people in the poor woodcutter's family. They were the woodcutter, his wife, and their three little girls.

Implied

2. Why did the oldest girl go into the woods to find her father? The oldest girl went into the woods to find her father because she was supposed to take him a warm dinner.

Literal

3. Why could the oldest girl not follow the grass seed that her father had used to show the way? The oldest girl could not follow the grass seed her father had left because the blackbirds had eaten it all up.

Implied

4. What did the father think was the reason the oldest girl could not follow the grass seed? The father thought that the reason the oldest girl could not follow the grass seed was that the grass seed was small and hard to see.

Literal

5. Where did each of the sisters go after she was lost? Each of the sisters went to a tiny house in the woods after she was lost.

Implied

6. Why did the old woman ask each sister to make supper and to make her beds? The old woman asked each sister to make supper and to make her bed because she was testing the girls to see who would be kind.

Literal

7. What happened to the first and second sister after they went to sleep? After the first and second sister went to sleep, the

old woman opened a large door in the floor, and they fell into the cellar.

Vocabulary

8. What is a cellar? A cellar is a room that is underground and is used mainly for storage.

Implied

9. Why did the youngest sister wake up in a castle instead of the cellar? The youngest sister woke up in a castle instead of a cellar because she was kind to the old woman and the animals. The youngest sister's kindness broke the spell, and the tiny house became a castle, the old woman became a princess, and the animals became the princess's servants.

Creative

10. What do you think will happen after the princess takes the three sisters to see their parents? (Accept creative answers.)

Use the following worksheet to review nouns and adjectives.

The phonics skill is the *cl* blend found in the words *clucked* and *clean*. Have your child think of more words with this blend. They may want to make a poster of the words they think of.

Answers: Accept adjectives, nouns, and page numbers from the story.

THE HOUSE IN THE WOODS, P. 111

Included in this folktale were many adjectives and nouns. Remember, an adjective describes a noun. A noun is a person, place, thing, or idea. See if you can make a list of some of the adjectives and nouns used in the story. Include the page number where you found the words. The first one has been done for you.

	adjective	*noun*	*page*
1.	poor	woodcutter	111
2.	_____	_____	_____
3.	_____	_____	_____
4.	_____	_____	_____
5.	_____	_____	_____
6.	_____	_____	_____
7.	_____	_____	_____
8.	_____	_____	_____
9.	_____	_____	_____
10.	_____	_____	_____

THE LAD WHO WENT TO THE NORTH WIND, p. 122

Preteach and review the following vocabulary: lad, pantry, spread, serve, crust, instead, true, believe, worth, making, fellow, bench, perhaps, and paid.

Answer the following comprehension questions on paper.

Vocabulary

1. What kind of meal did the North Wind keep taking from the boy? The North Wind kept taking the type of meal you use for cooking.

Literal

2. What did the boy do after the North Wind took the meal for the third time? After the North Wind took the meal for the third time, the boy went to the North Wind's house and asked for his meal back.

Implied

3. Was it wise for the boy to use the cloth while staying at the inn? Why or why not? It was not wise for the boy to use the cloth while staying at the inn because the innkeeper saw what it did and stole it.

Implied

4. Why did the boy not realize that his cloth was gone? The boy did not realize that his cloth was gone because the innkeeper put another piece of cloth by the boy when he took the boy's cloth.

Literal

5. How did the boy's mother react when he tried to use the cloth and it did not work? When the boy tried to use the cloth and it did not work, the boy's mother laughed at him.

Literal

6. What were the other two things the North Wind gave the boy to replace the meal? The North Wind gave the boy a ram that made money and a stick that would hit things by itself to replace the meal.

Implied

7. Why did the boy go back to the inn after he was given the third gift? The boy went back to the inn after he was given the third

gift because he figured out what had happened to the cloth and ram. He was going to use the stick to get the other two gifts back.

Implied

8. How did the boy find out for sure that the innkeeper was taking his gifts? The boy found out for sure that the innkeeper was taking his gifts by pretending to be asleep and watching the innkeeper trade his stick for another one.

Literal

9. What did the boy do with the cloth, ram, and stick after he left the inn? After he left the inn, the boy took the cloth, ram, and stick home.

Creative

10. What do you think the mother's reaction will be this time? Accept reasonable answers.

The phonics lesson is the *st* blend found in the words *stick, stop,* and *stayed.* Your child can look in another story to find more words with this blend.

Use the provided worksheet to practice pronouns.

Answers: 1. her   2. it or them   3. he   4. he or she   5. it   6. we   7. they   8. you

THE LAD WHO WENT TO THE NORTH WIND, p. 122

You already know that a noun is a person, place, thing, or idea. A pronoun is a word that takes the place of a noun. Pronouns are words like: *she, he, it, we, you, they,* and *them.* Instead of saying, "Pam went to the store," you could say, "She went to the store." Write an appropriate pronoun to complete each sentence.

1. The woman sent _____ only child to kitchen for some bread.

2. The child dropped _____ on the floor.

3. The boy wished _____ could fly his kite today.

4. My friend said that _____ and I could skate together.

5. The cat thought _____ could jump on top of the cabinet.

6. My parents decided that _____ would go on a vacation to the mountains.

7. I saw that _____ were almost ready to go.

8. Your mom thought that _____ might want to come with me.

THE MONTHS, p. 130

Preteach and review the following vocabulary: months, January, February, April, June, posies, July, August, September, golden-rod, pod, October, November, chilly, whirling, frost, December, and ends.

There are no comprehension questions for this poem.

This poem uses the terms *either* and *neither.* Use the provided worksheet to practice using these words correctly.

The phonics lesson is the *ow* sound found in the words *snow* and *showers.* Find more words in the poem that have the same vowel sounds as these two words.

Use the worksheet for an activity in rhyming words.

For an extension, have your child use the same rhyming pattern to write a poem about his or her favorite month.

Answers: Accept rhyming words for each.

THE MONTHS, p. 130

List five more words that rhyme with the words given.

snow   down   bee   rain

_____   _____   _____   _____

_____   _____   _____   _____

_____   _____   _____   _____

_____   _____   _____   _____

_____   _____   _____   _____

WHO HAS SEEN THE WIND?,

P. 131

Preteach the following vocabulary: nor and trembling.

There are no comprehension questions for this poem.

This poem uses the terms *either* and *neither.* Use the provided worksheet to practice using these words correctly.

The phonics lesson is the long *e* sound spelled with *ei.* The words *either* and *neither* are words that fit this description. Brainstorm other words like these or look in another story to find more words.

Answers: 1. either 2. neither 3. either 4. neither 5. either 6. either

WHO HAS SEEN THE WIND?, p. 131

This poem uses the words *either* and *neither*. Sometimes these words
   are confused in speaking and writing. *Either* means one or the
   other. Sometimes the word "or" is used in sentences with the
   word *either*. *Neither* means not one or the other. Sometimes the
   word "nor" is used with the word *neither*. Fill in the following
   sentences with the word that makes the most sense. Choose
   either or *neither*.

1. You have to choose. You may have _____ vanilla or
   chocolate ice cream?

2. Yuck, I want _____ spinach nor brussel sprouts!

3. Mommy is going to buy you one toy. You can choose _____
   this one or that one.

4. I got into trouble because I completed _____ of my
   chores.

5. Dad said we could eat _____ a hot dog or a
   hamburger.

6. _____ Quentin or Jeff may spend the night, but not
   both of them.

COME LITTLE LEAVES, p. 133

Preteach and review vocabulary: fluttering, content, earthy, and blanket.

There are no comprehension questions for this poem.

This is another rhyming poem. Use the worksheet for more practice with this skill.

The phonics lesson is the *wh* blend found in the words *whirling* and *white*. List more *wh* blend words.

Answer: Accept properly rhyming lines.

COME LITTLE LEAVES, p. 133

This poem has pairs of rhyming words. Complete this poem on school. Remember to make rhyming words for the words at the end of each line you are given.

School Days

I went to school one day

_____

During recess I will laugh and run

_____

In my class, I hoped to find,

_____

Now, try one on your own. Choose a subject you know a lot about. Make every two lines rhyme. Use the space here or on the back for your creative poem.

_____

_____

_____

_____

_____

_____

THE LEAF THAT WAS AFRAID,

P. 134

Preteach and review vocabulary: sigh, stopped, and colors.

Answer the following comprehension questions on paper.

Literal

1. What did the wind make the little leaf do when he talked to her? When the wind talked to the little leaf, he made her sigh and cry.

Implied

2. What color was the little leaf in the summer? How do you know? The little leaf was green in the summer because leaves are green in the summer, before they change colors in the fall.

Literal

3. How did the little leaf answer the wind when he asked her if she was ready to go? The little leaf told the wind that she was ready to fly away with the other leaves when the wind asked her if she was ready to go.

Implied

4. What does the story mean when it says the little leaf fell asleep? When the story says the little leaf fell asleep, it probably means the leaf started decomposing.

Creative

5. Why do you think this story was written? Accept reasonable answers.

Use the worksheet to review the *wh* blend and practice the *wr* blend.

Answers: 1. why or wry 2. where 3. wring 4. who 5. writing 6. wrong 7. wrist 8. whole 9. whip 10. while 11. which 12. wrinkle

THE LEAF THAT WAS AFRAID, P. 134

Make words by using the *wr* and the *wh* blends. Use the dictionary to check your words.

1. _____y

2. _____ere

3. _____ing

4. _____o

5. _____iting

6. _____ong

7. _____ist

8. _____ole

9. _____ip

10. _____ile

11. _____ich

12. _____inkle

THE SNOW MAN, P. 136

Preteach and review vocabulary: simply, pale-faced, frozen, few, completely, faithful, and apart.

There are no comprehension questions for this poem.

Use the worksheet for a lesson on facts and opinions.

The phonics lesson is the *sn* blend found in the word *snowman*. Discover more words with the *sn* blend.

Answers:
1. F 2. O 3. F 4. F 5. O 6. F 7. O 8. O 9. O 10. F 11. F 12. O
1. flies 2. buggies 3. cries 4. babies 5. ladies

THE SNOW MAN, p. 136

Facts are things that can be proven. For example, you can prove that Nebraska is one of the fifty states by looking it up in an encyclopedia. Opinions are decisions or judgments that cannot be proven. For example, *"Nebraska is the most boring state I have ever visited."* This is an opinion because it cannot be proven that Nebraska is a boring state, and another person may think Nebraska is an exciting state. Read the following sentences about snow and snowmen. Decide whether the statement is a fact or an opinion. Put F for fact or O for opinion.

1. ____ Warm weather will melt a snowman.

2. ____ Building snowmen is fun.

3. ____ A snowman is made of frozen water.

4. ____ Water freezes at 32 degrees Fahrenheit.

5. ____ Making snow angels are more exciting than throwing snowballs.

6. ____ You can make snowballs out of snow.

7. ____ Igloos are the worst type of house to live in.

8. ____ A carrot makes the best nose for a snowman.

9. ____ The most creative snowmen are built by kids.

10. ____ You can check the temperature outside with a thermometer.

11. ____ When the temperature rises, the snowman will melt.

12. ____ Eskimos are foolish for living in igloos.

THE DOLLS' THANKSGIVING DINNER, p. 138

Preteach and review the following vocabulary: Polly, clothes, broom, vase, napkins, plate, Susan, pink, Dora, Jane, Hannah, careful, knife, teaspoon, carved, meat, potato, cranberry, sauce, squash, pie, dessert, raisins, visitors, scattered, front, steps, and moment.

Answer the following comprehension questions on paper.

Literal

1. What did Polly Pine ask her mother? Polly Pine asked her mother why her dolls couldn't have a Thanksgiving dinner as well as little girls.

Implied

2. How old do you think Polly Pine is? Why? Polly Pine is probably between six and ten years old because she is young enough to pretend with dolls, yet she is old enough to dress her dolls and set up her dollhouse.

Implied

3. How did Polly Pine feel when her mother made Thanksgiving dinner for her dolls? Polly Pine felt very excited and happy when her mother made Thanksgiving dinner for her dolls.

Literal

4. Who was Polly Pine having dinner with on Thanksgiving? Polly Pine was having dinner with her parents and some friends on Thanksgiving.

Literal

5. Who went with Polly to see if the dolls liked their dinner? Everyone went with Polly to see if the dolls liked their dinner.

Implied

6. How do you think everyone felt when they saw that the dolls' dinner had been eaten? When everyone saw that the dolls' dinner had been eaten, they felt very surprised. They were surprised because they knew the dolls could not have eaten the dinner.

Literal

7. Who really ate the dolls' Thanksgiving dinner? It was three mice that ate the dolls' Thanksgiving dinner.

Implied

8. Why did Mother ask if she should get the cat? Mother asked if she should get the cat because the cat would catch and kill the mice.

Literal

9. Why did Father tell Mother not to get the cat? Father told Mother not to get the cat because he thought the poor little mice should have Thanksgiving dinner just like them.

Creative

10. What kind of special Thanksgiving dinner would you like to prepare and who would you invite? Accept reasonable answers.

Use the provided worksheet for a creative writing lesson.

The phonics lesson is the consonant blends of *dr* and *br*. Have your child find words in the story that begin with these blends.

Answers: Accept ability appropriate writing.

THE DOLLS' THANKSGIVING DINNER, P. 138

Everyone has had a memorable holiday. Think about a special holiday you have had. Fill in the blanks and follow other directions to write about your special holiday.

1. My special holiday was _____.
2. Draw three pictures to show why this holiday was extra special. In the spaces next to each picture, write about your picture.

A.

_____

_____

_____

_____

_____

_____

_____

B.

_____

_____

_____

_____

_____

_____

C.

_____

_____

_____

_____

_____

_____

THE GOLDEN COBWEBS, p. 143

Preteach and review the following vocabulary: cobwebs, trimmed, popcorn, candies, toys, locked, already, canary, spider, attic, poke, single, busy, halls, teeny, crawly, trumpet, face, and wand.

Answer the following comprehension questions on paper.

Implied

1. What month does this story take place? How do you know? This story takes place in December because it is just before Christmas, and Christmas is in December.

Literal

2. Why were the doors of the room locked? The doors of the room were locked so that the children could not get in and see the Christmas tree.

Vocabulary

3. The tree was trimmed with popcorn, candles, toys, and other items. What does trimmed mean? When the story says the tree was trimmed with popcorn, candles, toys, and other items, it means the tree was decorated with those things.

Implied

4. Do you think the setting of this story is the past, present, or future? Why? The setting of this story is the past because they used candles instead of electric lights. Another reason it is set in the past is that the house mother would not let the children see the tree before Christmas day, which is an old tradition that most people no longer observe.

Literal

5. The spiders were very sad because they had not seen the Christmas tree. Who helped them solve their problem? When the spiders were very sad because they had not seen the Christmas tree, the Christmas Fairy helped them solve their problem.

Literal

6. What did the spiders do after they went in to see the Christmas tree? After the spiders went in to see the Christmas tree, they crawled all over the Christmas tree and left cobwebs everywhere.

Literal

7. What were some of the toys that were hung on the tree? A doll, drum, trumpet, and jumping jack were some of the toys hung on the tree.

Implied

8. Were the children who lived in the house girls, boys, or both? The children who lived in the house were probably both girls and boys because of the types of toys on the tree.

Implied

9. Why did the Christmas Fairy turn the spider webs into golden cobwebs? The Christmas Fairy turned the spider webs into golden cobwebs because she knew the children would be upset about spider webs all over the tree, but golden cobwebs would make a beautiful decoration.

Creative

10. Do you think the Christmas Fairy will help the spiders see the tree next year? Why or why not? (Accept reasonable answers.)

Use the provided worksheet to review the parts of speech.

The phonics lesson is the consonant blends *cr* as in *creepy* and *chr* as in *Christmas*. These words have the same beginning sound but have different spellings. Look in the dictionary for more words with each type of spelling.

Answers: Accept reasonable answers from the story.

THE GOLDEN COBWEBS, P. 143

A noun is a person, place, thing, or idea. An adjective describes a noun. A verb tells us what the noun is doing. Look back in your story and list some of the nouns, adjectives, and verbs you can find.

adjectives	nouns	verbs
1. _____	_____	_____
2. _____	_____	_____
3. _____	_____	_____
4. _____	_____	_____
5. _____	_____	_____
6. _____	_____	_____
7. _____	_____	_____
8. _____	_____	_____
9. _____	_____	_____
10. _____	_____	_____

THE EASTER RABBIT, P. 149

Preteach and review the following vocabulary: waved, lonely, blossoms, dare, steal, besides, timid, bunny's, hippity-hop, quiet, tracks, and message.

Answer the following comprehension questions on paper.

Literal

1. Why did the children go to the woods? The children went to the woods to see if spring had come yet.

Implied

2. When spring came, why did the children not come to the woods? The children did not go to the woods when spring came because they did not know that spring had come.

Literal

3. Why would the robin not go tell the children? The robin would not go tell the children because she was busy building her nest.

Literal

4. Which animal finally agreed to go tell the children that spring was here? The rabbit agreed to go tell the children that spring was here.

Vocabulary

5. Use the word *timid* in a sentence. Accept reasonable sentences.

Implied

6. Why did the animals make a big basket from twigs and leaves? The animals made a big basket from twigs and leaves so the rabbit could carry the eggs and flowers for the children.

Implied

7. Why did the bunny leave a nest with an egg on the doorstop instead of someplace else? The bunny left a nest with an egg on the doorstep instead of someplace else because he wanted the children to see the nest and know that spring had come as soon as they came outside.

Literal

8. How did the children know that the rabbit had brought the message about spring? The children knew that the rabbit had

brought the message about spring because they saw the tracks from the rabbit's feet.

Implied

9. Why were the children so excited about spring? The children were so excited about spring because it was the end of cold weather, and they could go into the woods and see the animals and their babies, flowers coming up, and tree buds bursting.

Creative

10. Tell about an enjoyable Easter or spring experience you have had.

Use the provided worksheet to do an animal research.

The phonics skill is the *fr* blend found in the word *frost*. Think of more words with the same consonant blend.

Answers: Help your child find the correct answers on his or her animal.

THE EASTER RABBIT, p. 149

This story has many different animals as characters. There is a rabbit, bird, squirrel, fox, bear, and dog. Think of an animal that you would like to know more about. Travel to the library and see if you can find some information on your animal.

Animal: _____

Description of animal:_____

_____

_____

Where does the animal live? _____

_____

What does it eat? _____

_____

How many babies or eggs does your animal have at one time? _____

_____

What are your animal's enemies? _____

_____

Additional information about your animal: _____

_____

_____

AMERICA, p. 154

There are no new vocabulary words for this poem.

There are no comprehension questions for this poem.

The phonics lesson is the long *i* sound spelled with a *y* as in the words *my* and *thy* in the poem. See how many other words you can find that have the same vowel sound spelled with a *y*.

Use the worksheet on synonyms and antonyms.

Answers: Accept other reasonable answers.

rapture—joy, swell—enlarge, awake—alert, silent—quiet, sound—noise, sad—unhappy, freezing—hot, loud—quiet, joyous—sad, alive—dead, meek—outgoing, deny—allow

AMERICA, p. 154

Synonyms are words that mean the same or nearly the same as other
words. An example is: *happy* and *glad*. See if you can discover
some synonyms to the following words.

Rapture _____

Swell _____

Awake _____

Silent _____

Sound _____

Sad _____

Antonyms are words that mean the opposite of other words. An example
is: hot and cold. Give the antonyms of the words below.

Freezing _____

Loud _____

Joyous _____

Alive _____

Meek _____

Deny _____

You may use a dictionary if you like.

THE FLAG, p. 155

There are no new vocabulary words for this poem.

There are no comprehension questions for this poem.

Research Betsy Ross and do a short report on the outlined worksheet.

The phonics skill is the *sk* consonant blend found in the word *sky*. Make a poster of other words that begin with the *sk* blend.

Answers: 1. sew the American flag 2. 1776 3. 13, the colonies 4. red, white 5. George Washington

THE FLAG, p. 155

Betsy Ross is an important person in history. Research and find out what she did that was important. Fill in the lines with your new information.

1. Betsy Ross was the first person to _____

_____.

2. This happened in the year _____.

3. The first American flag had _____ stars that stood for

_____.

4. It also had _____ and _____ stripes.

5. Betsy Ross had a pew in church next to _____

_____.

Do your own drawing of Betsy Ross's flag.

JOAN AND PIERRE, p. 156

Preteach and review the following vocabulary: Joan, Pierre, French, village, torn, St. Nicholas, shoes, salute, American, trenches, hats, pair, brother, and Junior.

Answer the following comprehension questions on paper.

Implied

1. In what country did Joan and Pierre live? Joan and Pierre lived in France because the story said they were French children.

Implied

2. Why had Joan and Pierre not seen each other for a long time? Joan and Pierre had not seen each other for a long time because World War One had destroyed their village, and they probably could not find each other.

Literal

3. Where did Pierre think that Joan had gotten her new coat? Pierre thought that Joan had gotten her new coat from St. Nicholas.

Implied

4. Where did Joan get her coat? Joan got her coat from the Junior Red Cross.

Literal

5. What else did Joan get from there? Joan also got a cap and food from the Junior Red Cross.

Literal

6. Why did Pierre want to know where Joan got her coat and food? Pierre wanted to know where Joan got her coat and food because he was cold and hungry.

Literal

7. What did the house have on top of it? The house had an American flag and a Red Cross flag on top of it.

Vocabulary

8. What part of a flag is the field? The field of a flag is the space where the designs are drawn.

Implied

9. Why did the boys and girls of America send things to the

French boys and girls? The American boys and girls sent things to the French boys and girls because the American children knew that the French children had lost all their things in the war, and the American children wanted to help.

Creative

10. What things do you think Pierre's little brother will be given when Pierre brings him to visit the Junior Red Cross? (Accept reasonable answers.)

All of the long and short vowel sounds have been covered. This would be an opportune time to review the long vowel sounds. Make a chart or separate lists of words brainstormed in each category.

Use the worksheet to learn about making nouns and verbs agree.

For an extension, look up the Red Cross for more information.

Answers: 1. is 2. are 3. am 4. is 5. was 6. were 7. were 8. was 9. will be 10. will

JOAN AND PIERRE, p. 156

It is important when you are writing to make sure your nouns and verbs agree in a sentence. Look at the following examples:

	Singular	Plural
Present:	I am happy.	We are happy.
Past:	I was happy.	We were happy.
Future:	I will be happy.	We will be happy.

Present Tense: Fill in the blanks with the correct verb. Use *am*, *is*, and *are*.

1. He _____ a great student because he studies.

2. They _____ going to the football game.

3. I _____ not supposed to ride with strangers.

4. The flag _____ a symbol for the United States.

Past Tense: Use *was* and *were*.

5. He _____ going to play soccer.

6. They _____ trying to spend the night in the tent.

7. They _____ at the grocery store to purchase bread.

8. What _____ the reason for you being late?

Future Tense: Use *will* and/or *be*.

9. Our family _____ _____ traveling to

   the mountains.

10. The team _____ win the championship if they win

    today.

LINCOLN AND HIS DOG, P. 160

Preteach and review the following vocabulary: Abe, cabin, family, sold, soil, railroads, wagons, furniture, oxen, sank, hubs, trotted, chase, floated, distance, coax, weight, freeze, cruel, shines, waded, shivering, and presidents.

Answer the following comprehension questions on paper.

Literal

1. What did Abraham Lincoln's friends call him? Abraham Lincoln's friends called him Abe.

Literal

2. Why did Abe's father decide to move his family? Abe's father decided to move his family because their farm had poor soil, and the father could not make a very good living.

Implied

3. Why did Abe's family move at the end of winter instead of waiting until later? Abe's family moved at the end of winter instead of waiting until later because they needed to get to the new farm and plant the spring crops.

Implied

4. Why did Abe's family use oxen rather than horses to pull the wagon? Abe's family used oxen rather than horses to pull the wagon because oxen are much stronger than horses, and oxen can endure harsher weather than horses.

Vocabulary

5. The story describes the oxen as faithful. What does faithful mean? Faithful means that the oxen were loyal to the family and would work hard.

Literal

6. Why did the little dog not cross the stream with everyone else? The little dog did not cross the stream when everyone else did because he had chased a rabbit far into the woods and was not at the stream when everyone else crossed.

Implied

7. Why did Abe take his shoes and stockings off even though the water was very cold? Abe took his shoes and stockings off even though the water was very cold because he wanted to have dry shoes and stockings to wear after he had saved the dog.

Implied

8. Why was the little dog shivering even though he was not in the water? The little dog was shivering even though he was not in the water because he was scared.

Literal

9. Why did the little dog keep close to Abe? The little dog kept close to Abe because he had found out that a good friend is worth more than many squirrels.

Creative

10. How do you think the rest of the family felt about Abe going back to get the little dog? (Accept reasonable answers.)

The phonics lesson is the *dr* blend from the word *dreamed*.

Use the provided worksheet to practice the *sh, sl, st,* and *str* blends.

Answers:

1. storm 2. strum 3. sheet 4. sleet 5. slow 6. stare 7. string
8. sheep 9. shop 10. sloppy 11. stitch 12. stranger

LINCOLN AND HIS DOG, p. 160

Use the correct consonant blend word for each of the following definitions. Use *sh, sl, st,* or *str*.

1. _____ a period of heavy rain and thunder

2. _____ what you do with a guitar

3. _____ what you lay on at night

4. _____ frozen rain

5. _____ not fast

6. _____ to keep looking at something

7. _____ a long strip of twine

8. _____ animal that get sheared

9. _____ to search for something to buy

10. _____ not neat

11. _____ a loop formed by a needle and thread

12. _____ an unknown person

THE LITTLE COOK, p. 165

Preteach and review the following vocabulary: Betty, knit, coach, drawn, seat, crowds, welcome, fife, Robert, United States, shady, porch, stepped, curtsy, maid, rosy, kettle, fresh, slices, ham, and leaned.

Answer the following comprehension questions on paper.

Literal

1. How old was Betty? Betty was ten years old.

Literal

2. Why did Betty volunteer to stay home? Betty volunteered to stay home and keep the house so the others could go see George Washington.

Implied

3. Why did the little girls throw flowers before Washington and the little boys march to meet him? The little girls threw flowers and the little boys marched to meet Washington to honor him.

Implied

4. Why did Betty curtsy to the tall man when he reached her steps? Betty curtsied to the tall man when he reached her steps because she was being polite.

Literal

5. What did the tall man ask Betty to give him? The tall man asked Betty to give him some breakfast.

Vocabulary

6. Use the word *kettle* in a sentence. Accept correct usage of the word.

Implied

7. Why did Betty go to so much trouble making breakfast for the tall man? Betty went to so much trouble making breakfast for the tall man because she knew he was important, and she wanted to do an extra good job.

Literal

8. How did the tall man thank Betty for breakfast? The tall man thanked Betty for breakfast by giving her a kiss.

Implied

9. How did Betty see Washington before Robert did? Betty saw Washington before Robert did because the tall man was George Washington.

Creative

10. How do you think Betty's family will react when they hear what happened? (Accept reasonable answers.)

Use the provided worksheet for a review of the short vowels.

For an extension, do some research on George Washington. Use the computer for a quick reference.

Answers: Accept correct vowel sounds.

THE LITTLE COOK, P. 165
Use the chart to find at least 10 words with the given short vowel sounds. Choose a few words to illustrate at the bottom.

	short *a*	short *e*	short *i*	short *o*	short *u*
1.					
2.					
3.					
4.					
5.					
6.					
7.					
8.					
9.					
10.					

HOW BUTTERCUPS CAME, p. 170

Preteach and review the following vocabulary: robber and sprang. There are no comprehension questions for this story.

Use the worksheet to learn about homophones.

Answers: 1. way 2. grate 3. great 4. piece 5. would 6. through 7. peace 8. wood 9. threw 10. weigh

HOW BUTTERCUPS CAME, p. 170

Homophones are words that have the same sound but have different spellings and meanings. Fill in the blank with the word from the word box that makes the most sense.

piece peace would wood great grate through threw weigh way

1. Which _____ did my friends go?

2. Would you _____ the cheese for the tacos?

3. You did an absolutely _____ job on your project.

4. Bob and his sister split the last _____ of cake.

5. _____ you take the garbage out?

6. The little boy was scared to walk _____ the woods.

7. Let there be _____ on Earth.

8. Jill and her brother placed more _____ on the fire.

9. My dad _____ the ball farther than me.

10. At the fruit stand, mom will _____ the bananas.

DAISIES, p. 171

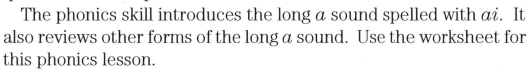

Preteach and review the following vocabulary: daisies, dot, and lady.

There are no comprehension questions for this poem.

The phonics skill introduces the long *a* sound spelled with *ai*. It also reviews other forms of the long *a* sound. Use the worksheet for this phonics lesson.

For an extension, make a nature bracelet by wrapping a piece of tape around your wrist with the sticky side facing out. Then take a nature walk and collect different bits of natural material to stick to your bracelet. When you get back, write about your outdoor adventure and the objects you collected for your nature bracelet.

Answers: Accept possible answers like:

a—away, sprang, way

ai—daisies, fair, train

a_e—came, tape, made

DAISIES, p. 171

The word *daisies* has the long *a* sound spelled with an *ai*. Fill in the chart with words you know that fit the long *a* description.

	a	ai	a_e
1.	_____	_____	_____
2.	_____	_____	_____
3.	_____	_____	_____
4.	_____	_____	_____
5.	_____	_____	_____

THE KIND OLD OAK, p. 172

Preteach and review the following vocabulary: plenty, violets, sheltered, storms, and taken.

Answer the following comprehension questions on paper.

Literal

1. What season was this story mostly about? This story was mostly about the season of winter.

Literal

2. How did the kind old oak help the violets? The kind old oak helped the violets by covering them with leaves to protect them from the cold.

Implied

3. Who was Jack Frost? Jack Frost is what people sometimes call winter.

Vocabulary

4. What are violets? Violets are small, low growing flowers with blue, purple, or white flowers.

Creative

5. What would you enjoy doing under an old oak tree? (Accept reasonable answers.)

Use the provided worksheet to practice the blends of *cr, fr dr,* and *pr.*

Answers: dream, project, Friday, afraid, cry, from, proud

THE KIND OLD OAK, p. 172

Let's add a few more blends to our writing. Use the following words to complete the paragraph. Each word will be used only once. Some words may not be used.

cry crept dream drop drip from afraid Friday proud project

During our weekly club meeting, my teacher was excited about a

_____ she had last night. She said it gave her an

idea for a fun activity. This new _____ would

be due next _____. I was _____

__ because I didn't know what to do. I felt like I was going to

_____. I went home and talked with my parents.

Finally, I got a great idea _____ my dad. I couldn't

wait to get started. This would be something I knew I would be

_____ of.

CLOVERS, P. 174

Preteach and review the following vocabulary: lawn, aside, fold, prayers, and dawns.

There are no comprehension questions for this poem.

The phonics lesson is a review of the short *u* sound found in the words *sun* and *up*. Do a word building activity to make new words with the *un* and *up* endings.

Use the worksheet to practice plural forms of words ending in *y*.

Answers: 1. prays 2. dries 3. plays 4. strays 5. monkeys 6. candies 7. skies 8. puppies 9. tries 10. toys

CLOVERS, p. 174

Words can be written in singular form, meaning one, or plural form, meaning more than one. If a word ends with a vowel + _y_, you just add an _s_. If a word ends with a consonant + _y_, you have to drop the _y_ and add _ies_. For example: _day_ would be changed to _days_ and _pry_ would be changed to _pries_. Change the following words to their plural forms.

1. pray _____

2. dry _____

3. play _____

4. stray _____

5. monkey _____

6. candy _____

7. sky _____

8. puppy _____

9. try _____

10. toy _____

THE GIRL WHO WAS CHANGED TO A SUNFLOWER, p. 175

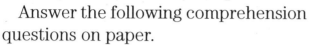

Preteach and review the following vocabulary: Clytie, water maiden, sea caves, Apollo's chariot, sun god, begins, heavens, western, leads, pranced, neither, tasted, slender, and petals.

Answer the following comprehension questions on paper.

Literal

1. Where did Clytie live? Clytie lived in the deep sea caves.

Implied

2. Why was Clytie's hair floating around her head? Clytie's hair was floating around her head because Clytie was in the water, and hair floats in the water.

Literal

3. Who was Apollo? Apollo was the sun god who rides the chariot of the sun across the sky.

Vocabulary

4. What is a chariot? A chariot is a decorated horse-drawn vehicle with two wheels.

Implied

5. How did Clytie feel about Apollo? Clytie must have liked Apollo, because she watched him a lot.

Literal

6. What direction did the flower turn to look at the sunset? The flower turned west to look at the sunset.

Implied

7. How was Clytie like a flower before she turns into one? Clytie is like a flower in the way she turned her face to the sun the same way plants follow the light.

Vocabulary

8. What does prance mean? Prance means to spring forward from the hind legs.

Vocabulary

9. Use *journey* in a sentence. Accept reasonable answers.

Creative

10. If you could be a flower, what kind would you be and why? (Accept creative answers.)

Use the provided worksheet for more practice on adjectives.

For an extension, research plants to determine the parts of the plant and the basic needs of plants. Also study the way plants move toward light.

Answers: Accept correct use of the ten adjectives.

THE GIRL WHO WAS CHANGED TO A SUNFLOWER, p. 175

This story includes many adjectives, which are descriptive words. Adjectives make your writing more interesting for the reader. Listed below are some of the adjectives included in the story. Use at least ten of these words to write your own imaginary story.

| beautiful tall shining pretty deep golden strange western |
| cool some strong sun bright wild slender |

_____

_____

_____

_____

_____

_____

_____

_____

_____

_____

_____

THE FAIRY SHOEMAKER, p. 179

Preteach and review the following vocabulary: Tom, elf, hammer, tiptoe, rip-rap, tick-a-tack-too, shrill, stitch, wrinkles, leather, apron, lap, snuffbox, ker-choo, sneezed, ditch, scarlet, stool, putting, whose, business, bogs, slipped, stumbled, pointing, dig, scarf, gay, hundreds, and beaten.

Answer the following comprehension questions on paper.

Literal

1. Why did Tom want to catch the fairy shoemaker? Tom wanted to catch the fairy shoemaker because he can tell Tom where there is a pot of gold.

Literal

2. Why did Tom's mother tell him he couldn't catch the fairy shoemaker? Tom's mother told Tom that the fairy shoemaker was tricky and would be gone if he looked away.

Implied

3. How did Tom's mother know that the fairy shoemaker was tricky? Tom's mother knew the fairy shoemaker was tricky because she probably tried to catch him when she was a little girl.

Literal

4. Where did Tom look for the fairy shoemaker every day? Tom looked on the hill, in the meadow, and in the woods to find the fairy shoemaker.

Implied

5. Why did the fairy shoemaker sing while he worked? The fairy shoemaker sang while he worked so someone would hear him and try to catch him. Accept other similar answers.

Vocabulary

6. Use meadow in a sentence. Accept reasonable sentences.

Literal

7. Why did Tom tie his yellow scarf around the tree? Tom tied his yellow scarf around the tree to mark it so he will know which one it was when he got back.

Vocabulary

8. What are wrinkles? Wrinkles are lines or folds in the skin of an old person.

Vocabulary

9. What are bogs? Bogs are areas that are wet and spongy.

Creative

10. How do you think Tom will earn his pot of gold by himself? (Accept reasonable answers.)

Palindromes are words or numbers that read the same backward and forward. An example of a palindrome is the word *noon*. For the phonics lesson, have fun finding palindromes in the last few stories.

Use the provided worksheet to learn about problems and solutions in stories.

Answers:

Problem—Tom wanted to catch the fairy shoemaker to find a pot of gold.

Solution—Tom fails to catch the fairy shoemaker and realizes that he must earn his own gold.

THE FAIRY SHOEMAKER, p. 179

In stories, usually there is a problem and a solution. A problem is the main thing that is wrong in the story. It is what the main character is struggling about. A solution is how the problem is solved. Tell the problem and solution for this story in the spaces below.

Problem—_____

_____

_____

Solution—_____

_____

_____

THE FIRST UMBRELLA, p. 190

Preteach and review the following vocabulary: umbrella, odd, thistledown, thick, toadstool, crept, and stem.

Answer the following comprehension questions on paper.

Literal

1. Describe the elf child. The elf child was little and wore a queer little coat, pointed cap, and tiny pointed shoes. His little ears were pointed too.

Implied

2. How do you know the elf had made a kite before? The elf had made a kite before because he seemed to know exactly what he was doing, like he had done it before. If this had been his first time, he would have had to try different objects to make the kite work.

Literal

3. Why didn't the elf want to get wet? The elf didn't want to get wet because he was wearing a new cap and coat.

Implied

4. Why was a toadstool a good place to get snug and dry? A toadstool was a good place to get snug and dry because it blocks the water and has a dry area underneath.

Literal

5. Why was the elf afraid of the mouse? The elf was afraid of the mouse because it may have eaten him.

Vocabulary

6. Use *sharp* in a sentence. Accept reasonable sentences.

Vocabulary

7. Use *crept* in a sentence. Accept reasonable sentences.

Creative

8. Besides a leaf or a toadstool, what else would make a good umbrella for the elf? Accept creative answers.

The phonics skill is the consonant blend *sq* from the word *squeak*. Think of a few more words with the same consonant blend.

Use the provided worksheet for creative writing.

Answers: Look for creativity as well as correct usage of capitalization and punctuation.

THE FIRST UMBRELLA, p. 190

This story is a tale of how the first umbrella came to be. Choose one of the following common objects and write your own tale of how you think it came to be. Use your imagination and add many details.

bicycle   shovel   doorknob   cane   scissors   wagon   fork   key   socks

_____

_____

_____

_____

_____

_____

_____

_____

_____

_____

_____

_____

THE TWELVE MONTHS, p. 193

Preteach and review the following vocabulary: twelve, Laura, Clara, hut, fretful, unkind, hate, pushed, wrapped, cloak, grapes, autumn, bunch, tore, strawberries, apronful, hurried, stored, potatoes, and beets.

Answer the following comprehension questions on paper.

Literal

1. Why did the old woman always let Clara do as she pleased? The old woman let Clara do as she pleased because Clara was cross and fretful just like the old woman.

Implied

2. Why did Laura let the old woman and Clara treat her this way? Laura was kind and gentle, and maybe she didn't think she has a choice.

Literal

3. How did Laura reply to Clara wanting violets? Laura said the violets were still asleep under the snow.

Implied

4. Why were the old men by the great fire in groups of three? The old men were in groups of three, because there are twelve months and four seasons. This makes three men for each season.

Implied

5. Why did the old men help Laura each time she needed help? The old men helped Laura because they knew she was kind and that she was sent out in the snow to get things that were impossible to get.

Literal

6. Why did the old woman and Clara go out into the forest? The old woman and Clara went to the forest for more apples.

Implied

7. Why didn't the old men give the old woman and Clara what they wanted? The old men didn't give the old woman and Clara what they wanted because they were cross and treated Laura in a bad way.

Vocabulary

8. What is a cloak? A cloak is a loose outer garment that covers.

Vocabulary

9. Use *wands* in a sentence. (Accept reasonable sentences.)

Creative

10. What is your favorite season and why? (Accept creative answers.)

The phonics skill is the consonant blend of *tw* from the word *twelve*. List more words that begin with *tw*.

Use the provided worksheet to practice sequencing.

Answers: 3, 5, 1, 2, 7, 6, 4

THE TWELVE MONTHS, p. 193

To sequence means to put events in order the way they happened. Put the following events from the story in the correct sequence. Put a 1 next to the event that happened first, a 2 next to the second event, and so on.

_____   Laura first meets the twelve men.

_____   The apples did not satisfy Clara, so she and the old woman went to get more.

_____   Clara and Laura moved in with an old woman after their parents died.

_____   Clara sent Laura to go find some violets.

_____   The twelve old men never forgot Laura and always took care of her.

_____   Clara and the old woman never found their home again.

_____   Laura walked to the twelve men to ask for strawberries.

THE MERMAN AND THE MERMAID, p. 204

Preteach and review the following vocabulary: merman, mermaid, bold, crow, throne, and pearl.

There are no comprehension questions for this poem.

Use the provided worksheet for a review of short and long vowel sounds.

Make a chart to compare and contrast the merman and the mermaid. Compare means to tell how they are alike. Contrast means to tell how they are different.

Answers: 1. short 2. long 3. long 4. long 5. long 6. short 7. short 8. long 9. short 10. long

THE MERMAN AND THE MERMAID, P. 204

Write "short" or "long" to tell the vowel sound found in the following words.

1. who _____

2. be _____

3. bold _____

4. sea _____

5. gold _____

6. her _____

7. curl _____

8. maid _____

9. man _____

10. throne _____

The Foolish Goose, p. 205

Preteach and review the following vocabulary: persons, caw, and lake.

Answer the following comprehension questions on paper.

Implied

1. Tell two ways this selection is written differently from the other stories that you have read recently. This is a play, the character's names are in front of what they are going to say, and there are directions to what the characters are supposed to do. Accept other reasonable answers.

Literal

2. Who are the characters in the play? The characters are Gray Goose, Wise Old Crow, White Crane, Brownie Hen, and a farmer.

Literal

3. How did Wise Old Crow trick Gray Goose? Wise Old Crow tricked Gray Goose by eating the corn he counted instead of making it go a long way.

Literal

4. What did Gray Goose say she hadn't seen before? Gray Goose hadn't seen pearls or diamonds before.

Implied

5. How did this play get its title? This play got this title because Gray Goose was foolish to get tricked three times.

Implied

6. Who helped Gray Goose the most? The farmer helped Gray Goose the most by telling him to put his corn in the ground.

Creative

10. What do you think Gray Goose will do with all the corn he grows? Accept reasonable answers.

For this play, use the provided worksheet to practice the story elements of setting, characters, problem, and solution.

Answers: Setting—The setting is a big road on a bright morning. Characters—Gray Goose, White Crane, Wise Old Crow, Brownie Hen, and a Farmer are the characters. Problem—The characters keep tricking Gray Goose and eating her corn. Solution—The Farmer tells Gray Goose to plant the corn. Gray Goose plants the corn, and now she has plenty.

THE FOOLISH GOOSE, p. 205

Story elements are the setting, characters, problem, and solution. Use the provided spaces to give the story elements for this play. Put your answers in complete sentences.

Setting: _____

_____

_____

Characters: _____

_____

_____

Problem: _____

_____

_____

Solution: _____

_____

_____

JACK AND THE BEANSTALK, p. 211

Preteach and review the following vocabulary: beanstalk, market, silk, queen, treasures, nurse, win, harp, thunder, finished, music, joyful, tune, ax, and crash.

Answer the following comprehension questions on paper.

Literal

1. Why did Jack's mother ask him to sell the cow? Jack's mother asked him to sell the cow to get money for bread.

Literal

2. Why was it foolish for Jack to trade the cow for the beans? It was foolish for Jack to trade the cow for the beans because he and his mother still had no money for bread.

Implied

3. Why did Jack think there must be food at the top of the beanstalk? Jack might have thought there would be food at the top of the beanstalk, because it had grown so fast, maybe there were other surprises to come.

Implied

4. Why did the fairy come when she did? The fairy came when she did so that she could catch Jack before he went to the great castle.

Literal

5. What had happened to Jack's father? The great giant had killed Jack's father, the king, and had taken all his treasures.

Implied

6. How would you describe the giant and how he acts? The giant is so heavy that the whole place shook, and he was very greedy and mean.

Vocabulary

7. What is a beanstalk? A beanstalk is a tall stem that beans grow on.

Vocabulary

8. Use *wand* in a sentence. Accept reasonable answers.

Implied

9. Why had Jack waited so long to go back to the castle for his father's harp? Jack probably waited so long to go back, because he and his mother had all the gold they needed.

Creative

10. If you had a magic harp, what would you do with it? (Accept creative answers.)

The phonics lesson is the consonant blends of *sp* and *sm*. Find some familiar words from the dictionary that have the same consonant blend.

For the activity, have your child write the next chapter of this story.

Answers: Check for correct capitalization and punctuation as well as creative writing.

JACK AND THE BEANSTALK, p. 211

In the last line of the story, the fairy tells Jack, "From this day on, you and your mother shall live in plenty." Think about what would happen if there was another chapter in this story. Write the next chapter. Tell about what is happening with Jack, his mother, and the magic harp.

_____

_____

_____

_____

_____

_____

_____

_____

_____

_____

_____

_____

The Little Tailor, p. 220

Preteach and review the following vocabulary: tailor, act, shop, fit, marry, questions, lie, courtiers, ink, paper, less, tongue, and teeth.

Answer the following comprehension questions on paper.

Literal

1. Why is Master Tailor so sad? Master Tailor is sad because the king was too upset to try on the coat he had taken to the castle.

Literal

2. Why does the king have to answer three questions? The king has to answer three questions to marry a beautiful princess.

Literal

3. Who asked the king the three questions? The father of the beautiful princess asked the three questions.

Implied

4. Why did the father of the beautiful princess ask the king these questions? The father of the beautiful princess wanted a wise man to marry his daughter.

Vocabulary

5. What is a courtier? A courtier is an assistant at a palace.

Implied

6. Why was Master Tailor surprised to see Little Tailor leave for the palace? Master Tailor was surprised to see Little Tailor go to the palace because he didn't believe Little Tailor had the right answers to the questions.

Vocabulary

7. Use *throne* in a sentence. Accept reasonable answers.

Implied

8. Why wasn't the king hungry? The king wasn't hungry because when you are sad or upset you usually don't feel like eating.

Implied

9. How can you tell that the king was excited about Little Tailor's answers? You can tell the king was excited because he said the answers were very good, he said this in great joy, and he was clapping his hands.

Creative

10. Write a question similar to the three questions in the play. Answer your question in a wise way, just like Little Tailor did. (Accept reasonable answers.)

Use the provided worksheet to practice letter writing.

Answers: Check the letter for the correct format.

THE LITTLE TAILOR, P. 220

In this play, the king is overjoyed when Little Tailor helps him answer three important questions. The king ends up marrying the beautiful princess due to the help he received from the tailor. Help the king write a letter of thanks to Little Tailor. Use the given format for the correct way to write a letter. Then copy your letter on another sheet of paper.

_____

date

Dear _____,

_____

_____

_____

_____

_____

_____

Sincerely,

_____

THE KING AND THE GOOSEHERD,

p. 227

Preteach and review the following vocabulary: gooseherd, books, park, read, tending, flock, order, schoolmaster, manage, whip, and swung.

Answer the following comprehension questions on paper.

Literal

1. What did the king love more than anything else in the world? The king loved books more than anything else in the world.

Implied

2. Why did the king send someone else to get the book from the park bench? The king sent someone else because he was too hot, and he had taken a long walk.

Implied

3. How did the gooseherd feel about the silver piece? The gooseherd's eyes sparkled, and he said that it was more than he made in a month tending geese.

Literal

4. Why did the gooseherd think the king could not tend the geese? The gooseherd said the king was too fat and too slow to watch over the sheep.

Implied

5. Why did the king think that he could tend the geese? The king thought that he could tend the geese because he was the king and could keep people in order.

Implied

6. Why didn't the king tell the gooseherd that he wasn't the schoolmaster? The king didn't tell the gooseherd that he wasn't the schoolmaster probably because telling that he was the king would have made the gooseherd treat him differently.

Vocabulary

7. What is a gander? A gander is a male goose.

Vocabulary

8. What would a shrill cry sound like? A shrill cry would be high pitched.

Implied

9. Why did the king help the gooseherd get the geese together again? The king was a good man and wanted to fix the

problem he caused.

Creative

10. What kind of books do you think the king liked to read? (Accept reasonable answers.)

Use the provided worksheet on silent letters.

Answers: 1. t, e 2. ea 3. gh 4. i 5. w, e 6. u, g 7. t 8. w, e 9. o 10. g 11. k 12. t

The King and the Gooseherd, p. 227

Some words have silent letters in them. We cannot hear the letter sound. Circle the silent letter or letters in each word.

1. castle
2. beautiful
3. thought
4. piece
5. answered
6. laughing
7. watch
8. whole
9. people
10. right
11. knew
12. stretch

THE RAINBOW, p. 233

Preteach and review the following vocabulary: rainbow, orange, wiped, sunbeams, and gowns.

There are no comprehension questions for this poem.

The phonics lesson is a review of the consonant blends found in this poem. Write the words with blends and circle the blend.

Use the following worksheet for a lesson on acrostics.

Answers: Accept reasonable acrostics.

THE RAINBOW, P. 233

Acrostics are fun to learn because they help us remember things. In an acrostic, each letter stands for a word. For example, look at the name *Roy G. Biv*. It is just a name until you know the secret. *Roy G. Biv* actually stands for *Red, Orange, Yellow, Green, Blue, Indigo,* and *Violet,* the colors of the rainbow. What about these letters? *M, V, E, M, J, S, U, N,* and *P* are the first letters of each of the nine planets. They may be difficult to remember in order this way, but what if we put these letters in a sentence? *My Very Educated Mother Just Served Us Nine Pizzas.* Can you come up with some acrostics to represent things you need to remember? What about the stages of the water cycle, the notes on a musical staff, or the continents?

_____

_____

_____

_____

_____

_____

_____

_____

_____

_____

How the Days Got Their Names, p. 234

Preteach and review the following vocabulary: lots, begun, Monday, Tuesday's, Tiu, spell, fear, Woden, wisdom, Wednesday, Thursday, Thor, lightning, Friday, Frigedaeg, Saturn, Saturday, and fifty.

Answer the following comprehension questions on paper.

Literal

1. Which god was the greatest? The greatest god was the sun.

Literal

2. What day was named after the god of war? Tuesday was named after the god of war.

Implied

3. How do we know that gods were important a long time ago? We know that the gods were important a long time ago, because the days were named after the gods.

Vocabulary

4. What does wisdom mean? Wisdom means being smart and having the ability to give sound advice.

Creative

5. Why do you think Saturday was a day of children's joy? (Accept reasonable answers.)

The phonics skill is the different sounds of *oo*. Use the worksheet for practice with this skill.

Answers:
moon—soon, loop, loot, boot, boom, cool, food, hoot
book—look, cook, good, wood, hook
door—floor
(accept other correct words)

HOW THE DAYS GOT THEIR NAMES, p. 234

There are several different sounds for the spelling *oo*. Listen to the different sounds of *oo* in the following words and find other words from this poem and some other stories that fit into each category.

moon	book	door
_____	_____	_____
_____	_____	_____
_____	_____	_____
_____	_____	_____
_____	_____	_____
_____	_____	_____
_____	_____	_____
_____	_____	_____
_____	_____	_____

WORD LIST

The following list contains the words of *Book Two* that were not taught in *Primer* or *Book One*. Many of these words have been developed phonetically in earlier lessons and are therefore not new to the child when read on the pages indicated. Such words are printed in italic type.

10	ready	19	*sparkling*		lazy
	path		diamonds		arrant
	pump		ago	26	candle
	nice		*shows*		quite
	clear		brave		grown-up
	bath	20	twinkle		past
11	*wood*pile		blazing		seem
	chips		*set*		*hard*
	cook		dew	27	lucky
12	rich		often		been
13	Top-knot		traveler		pay
	Biddy		though		*piece*
	scratching	21	half		shoulder
	new-laid		hour	28	*hot*
15	bathed		*band*		heavy
	dressed		danced		riding
	while		a-searching		rode
16	dipper		skies	29	foot
	thirsty		minute		load
	tin		course		*trade*
	dry	22	naughty		reins
17	sharp		*stood*	30	driving
	stones	23	toward		brought
	among		oho		sunny
	started	24	goes	31	clapped
	poured		use		drove
	hand		heels		*drop*
18	queer	25	funniest		*kicked*
	happened		proper		dust
	shining		which	32	butcher
	silver		shoots		wheelbarrow
	drink		India-rubber		*killed*
	shone		*ball*		beef
	feel		none		pork
			buttercup		

33 troubles
carrying
stolen
thief
throw

34 *rid*
scissors-grinder
pocket

35 either
answered

36 done
need
grindstone

37 bank
stooped
watched

38 charmingly
curled
heath
week

39 folks
terribly
changed
paint
washed
arm's
trodden
least
sake

40 grasshopper
same
worker

41 *harm*
stiff

42 frog
ox
animal
herself
strange
young

43 burst
silly

44 pleasing
everybody
taking
donkey
easier
ashamed

45 women
selfish
room
enough
able
pole
carried

46 untied
drive
nobody

47 *manger*
ought
starve
life
else

48 *strangers*

49 fur
mine
quick

50 gentle
speak
sound
purr-r
danger
dreadful
most

51 listen
chin
moved
wild
stretched

52 squee-hee-hee
mind
fierce
remember
deeds

53 cream
apple-tart
wanders
lowing
stray
blown
pass
showers

54 Taro
turtle
fisherman
teased
teasing

55 stroked
thousand
boat

56 saving
sea king's
palace
bottom

57 bloomed
gatekeeper
helpers
princess

60 yesterday
saved
share

59 elephant
monkey
quarrel
climb
agree
pick

60 trunk

61 *stream*
neither
strength
quickness
gathered

62 bear
soldier
tame

march
really
inn
upstairs
gun

63 tramp
snuffed
rat-a-tat-tat
hold

64 left
led

65 sparrow
bleat
teach
taught

66 afterwards
sheepfold
late

67 *tapped*
breakfast

68 swallow
sun-loving
hurrying
o'er
certain
cloudy
follow

69 cakes
baking
wore
cape
cap
those
dough

70 oven

71 *wood*pecker

72 secret
cherry

73 shan't
whole

74 weather
skates

sleds
honey-bees
hum
pussies
willow-*trees*

75 magpie
lesson
mud
shape
thrush
sticks

76 twigs
wind
lining
suits
lined
alike

77 porcupine

78 *hog*
sitting

79 *tight*
knocked

81 ram
fed
mutton
against
struck

82 *free*
kindness
feed
ourselves

83 meal
roasted

84 live
gabbling
moss
farther

85 soup
wealthy

86 snug

87 wolves

neighbors
expecting
snapped
nipped
pecked
giant

88 witch
snipped

89 Atri
wrong
tower
bell rope
ring
judges
punish

90 *rang*
robes
rung
thin
ding-dong

91 *nap*

92 *lame*
almost
blind
starving
belongs
castle

93 war
wherever
unless
bad
shame
word

94 stable

95 summer-maker
season
ice
bare
Ojeeg
Indian
deer
feast

96 *bow*
arrow
fingers
numb
use
wigwam
magic

97 *meet*
tears
smiled
fond
son

98 otter
beaver
badger
journey
mountain
touched

99 jumper
breath
rock

100 fists
breeze
rushed

101 melted
sparkled
since

102 earn
living
straw

103 huff
rap

104 third
bricks

106 *rows*
juicy
o'clock

107 these

108 *fair*
churn
bought
except

110 *heat*
lid
visit

111 *wood*cutter
wife
lose
noon

112 lifted
latch
hearth
speckled

113 meant
kitchen
dish
stew

114 large
bump
cellar

115 sent
tomorrow

116 hoot

117 peas

118 spoke
armful
clean
sheets

119 ivory
chairs
pinched
center
table
servants

120 surprised

122 *lad*
pantry

123 spread
serve

124 *crust*

125 instead
true
believe

126 worth

127 making
fellow

128 bench
perhaps

129 paid

130 months
January
February
April
June
posies
July
August
September
golden-rod
pod
October

131 November
chilly
whirling
frost
December
ends
nor
trembling

133 fluttering
content
earthy
blanket

134 sigh
stopped
colors

136 simply
pale-faced
frozen

137 *few*
completely
faithful
apart

138 Polly
clothes
broom
vase
napkins
plate

139 Susan
pink
Dora
Jane
Hannah
careful
knife
teaspoon

140 carved
meat
potato
cranberry
sauce
squash
pie

141 dessert
raisins
visitors
scattered

142 front
steps
moment

143 cobwebs
trimmed
popcorn
candies
toys
locked
already
canary

144 spider
attic
poke
single

145 busy
halls

146 *teeny*
crawly

147 *trumpet*
face

148 wand

149 waved

150 lonely
blossoms

151 dare
steal
besides
timid

152 bunny's
hippity-hop
quiet

153 *tracks*
message

156 Joan
Pierre
French
village
torn
St. Nicholas

157 shoes

158 salute
American
trenches
hats
pair
brother

159 Junior

160 Abe
cabin
family
sold
soil

161 railroads
wagons
furniture
oxen

sank
hubs

162 trotted
chase
floated

162 distance
coax
weight
freeze
cruel
whines
waded

164 shivering
presidents

165 Betty
knit
coach
drawn
seat

166 crowds
welcome
fife
Robert

167 United States
shady
porch
stepped
curtsy

168 *maid*
rosy
kettle
fresh

169 *slices*
ham
leaned

170 robber
sprang

171 daisies
dot
lady

172 plenty
violets

sheltered
storms

173 taken

174 lawn
aside
fold
prayers
dawns

175 Clytie
watermaiden
sea caves
Apollo's chariot
sun god
begins
heavens

176 western
leads

177 pranced
neighed
tasted

178 slender
petals

179 Tom
elf
hammer
tiptoe

180 *rip-rap*
tick-a-tack-too
shrill
stitch

181 wrinkles

182 leather
apron
lap
snuffbox

183 ker-choo
sneezed

184 ditch

185 scarlet
stool

putting
whose
business

186 *bogs*
slipped
stumbled

187 pointing
dig
scarf

188 *gay*

189 hundreds
beaten

190 umbrella
odd
thistledown
thick

191 *toadstool*
crept
stem

193 twelve
Laura
Clara
hut
fretful
unkind
hate

194 pushed
wrapped
cloak
grapes
autumn

196 bunch
tore
strawberries

199 apronful

200 hurried

203 *stored*
potatoes
beets

204 merman
mermaid

bold
crow
throne
pearl

205 persons

207 caw
lake

211 beanstalk
market

213 silk

214 queen
treasures
nurse
win

215 harp
thunder
finished

218 music
joyful
tune

219 ax
crash

220 tailor
act
shop
fit

221 marry
questions

222 *lie*

223 courtiers

224 ink
paper

225 less

226 tongue
teeth

227 gooseherd
books
park
read

tending
flock

228 order
schoolmaster
manage

229 *whip*
swung

233 rainbow
orange
wiped

sunbeams
gowns

234 *lots*
begun
Monday

235 Tuesday's
Tiu
spell
fear
Woden

wisdom
Wednesday

236 Thursday
Thor
lightning
Friday
Frigedaeg
Saturn
Saturday
fifty

Books Available from
Lost Classics Book Company
American History

Stories of Great Americans for Little Americans .... Edward Eggleston
A First Book in American History .... Edward Eggleston
A History of the United States and Its People .... Edward Eggleston

Biography
The Life of Kit Carson .... Edward Ellis

English Grammar
Primary Language Lessons .... Emma Serl
Intermediate Language Lessons .... Emma Serl

(Teacher's Guides available for each of these texts)

Elson Readers Series
Complete Set .... William Elson, Lura Runkel, Christine Keck
The Elson Readers: Primer .... William Elson, Lura Runkel
The Elson Readers: Book One .... William Elson, Lura Runkel
The Elson Readers: Book Two .... William Elson, Lura Runkel
The Elson Readers: Book Three .... William Elson
The Elson Readers: Book Four .... William Elson
The Elson Readers: Book Five .... William Elson, Christine Keck
The Elson Readers: Book Six .... William Elson, Christine Keck
The Elson Readers: Book Seven .... William Elson, Christine Keck
The Elson Readers: Book Eight .... William Elson, Christine Keck

(Teacher's Guides available for each reader in this series)

Historical Fiction
With Lee in Virginia .... G. A. Henty
A Tale of the Western Plains .... G. A. Henty
The Young Carthaginian .... G. A. Henty
In the Heart of the Rockies .... G. A. Henty
For the Temple .... G. A. Henty
A Knight of the White Cross .... G. A. Henty
The Minute Boys of Lexington .... Edward Stratemeyer
The Minute Boys of Bunker Hill .... Edward Stratemeyer
Hope and Have .... Oliver Optic
Taken by the Enemy, First in *The Blue and the Gray Series* .... Oliver Optic
Within the Enemy's Lines, Second in *The Blue and the Gray Series* .... Oliver Optic
On the Blockade, Third in *The Blue and the Gray Series* .... Oliver Optic
Stand by the Union, Fourth in *The Blue and the Gray Series* .... Oliver Optic
Fighting for the Right, Fifth in *The Blue and the Gray Series* .... Oliver Optic
A Victorious Union, Sixth and Final in *The Blue and the Gray Series* .... Oliver Optic
Mary of Plymouth .... James Otis

For more information visit us at: http://www.lostclassicsbooks.com